Of This Time, of That Place

and Other Stories

THE WORKS OF LIONEL TRILLING

UNIFORM EDITION

LIONEL TRILLING

OF THIS TIME, OF THAT PLACE

and Other Stories

Selected by Diana Trilling

A HARVEST/HBJ BOOK

HARCOURT BRACE JOVANOVICH

NEW YORK AND LONDON

Printed in the United States of America

Library of Congress Cataloging in Publication Data

Trilling, Lionel, 1905–1975.
Of this time, of that place, and other stories.

(The Works of Lionel Trilling)
(A Harvest/HBJ book)
CONTENTS: Impediments.—The other Margaret.—
Notes on a departure.—[etc.]
I. Trilling, Diana.   II. Title.
III. Series: Trilling, Lionel, 1905–1975. Works.
[PZ3.T73Of 1980]   [PS3539.R56]   813'.52   80-14022
ISBN 0-15-668062-9

First Harvest/HBJ edition 1980
A B C D E F G H I J

Contents

Of This Time, of That Place

and Other Stories

Impediments

(From *The Menorah Journal*, 1925)

Let me not to the marriage of true minds
Admit impediments. . . .

IF you sit next to a man in class and if, in a bashfully forward sort of way, he insists upon whispering during the lecture a series of ironic comments on the professor's capabilities, and if, when the notebooks have snapped shut and the cigarettes are being lighted, he suggests accompanying you to your next class, you can only be polite enough to smile at the comments, offer him a cigarette and hold up your end of the conversation as you cross the campus. Hettner forced me to these perfunctory courtesies. I did not like the fellow, a scrubby little Jew with shrewd eyes and full, perfect lips that he twisted out of their crisply cut shape. He was puzzled and morose, writhing beneath a depression which he tried to brighten by a humor intended for the piquant and extravagant, but never succeeding, and in its failure darkening still more the shabby sable that shrouded him. That there was something wrong with Hettner it was easy to suppose, with his soul probably, a matter in which I had no great concern.

The distance that we walked between our two halls was short enough to confine our conversations to the fewest of subjects, and these I was careful to make the most impersonal. I felt always defensive against some attempt Hettner might make to break down the convenient barrier I was erecting against men who were too much of my own race and against men who were not of my own race and hated it. I feared he would attempt to win into the not-too-strong tower that I had built myself, a tower of contemptible ivory perhaps, but very useful. He never, it is true, offered any overt sign that might indicate a desire to further our slight acquaintance, nor did he force upon me any confidences that might have been obnoxious, but there was a straining eagerness about him, an uncertain fugitive air that put me on my guard lest he come to me for a refuge I did not want to give. And so I was careful that we talked always of the lecturer, agreeing that he was a dry enough stick, whom, however, I could not find it in myself to condemn on the score of an utter absorption in barren and meaningless fact. I wanted facts, quite lonely, quite cold, quite isolated facts that I could juggle and rearrange for myself into novel and useful relations. But Hettner, whose reading and knowledge were wider than mine, whose appetite was more varied and whose capacity more commodious, who devoured what he tasted and retained what he devoured with apparently never a single *katharsis,* had not my—more elementary perhaps—desire and wanted the links of his relations ready forged for him.

In the three days of the week that we saw each other our total conversation could not have exceeded fifteen minutes. I did not find these minutes difficult; I had only to repeat my previous opinion in different terms, a little more portentously or a little more flippantly, and I found it good dialectical exercise. Hettner, however, was quite serious; if his irony be discounted, he was serious about everything. This irony of his was a curious and incongruous stroke in the composition of the man; it threw him a little out of drawing. Essentially, despite the quickness and vigor of his mind, he was very humble, afraid, out of the larger picture. He talked and scoffed because he did not dare shut up, and his talk was an insistent and arrogant apology for his existence.

I did not mind the fifteen minutes a week that I afforded him. There are times when one rather enjoys offering a constrained politeness, and it was amusing to ward off this puzzled soul as it groped faintly after me. I thought, however, that there was no reason for an uninvited and unreasonable call at my room. Early in the evening I had taken a shower and reconciled myself to the composition of a long term-paper on Browning. It was not an unpleasant task; I knew that it was not required of me to engage in the difficult job of saying what I wanted to say. I had only to use the familiar formula and my resulting pages would be quite acceptable and far more painlessly achieved: a few paragraphs of discreet eulogy, very graceful, a cursory re-reading of the important poems with discreet comment, a discreet closing criticism with a discreet prophecy that the poet will be read more and more as the years wend their unswerving course, and a discreet use throughout of the words *prolix, over-clever, warped, palpitant* and *dramatic.*

It was well after eleven before I felt sleepy, with nearly four hours of writing before me. A cup of strong tea, I thought, might clear my head, and I set a pot boiling on an electric grill and continued with my work. The water had begun to steam when Hettner knocked.

"Are you busy?" he asked.

Now, if it had been anyone else, I would have replied, "Hell, yes. I have to finish this damned thing before morning. Get out!" I would have said it with a gruff severity that anyone would have understood for facetious, but I doubted Hettner's ability to catch even that obvious humor. There was a crudeness and awkwardness about him that would have made him construe it as downright discourtesy. So I said, "Not with anything of importance," which was true enough.

I offered him a chair. He took it. I gave him a cigarette. He pursed up his lips round and placed it between them. He was unskilful at drawing up the smoke; instead he blew out through the cigarette and extinguished the match I held up for him. I struck another, and when I had put a tip of flame to the slender tube he mouthed so clumsily, I turned to see if the tea had sufficiently brewed. An exclamation of pained annoyance escaped from him. He had neglected to moisten the end of his cigarette, its rice paper had stuck to his upper lip and when he had pulled it from his mouth he had taken off a piece of skin. A small patch of bloody flesh showed on his dry lip and he moistened it with his tongue.

I handed him a cup of tea.

"Will you have sugar? We don't provide lemon or cream at this poor inn." I was doing the politely trivial, and though I was being very fatuous at it, I was determined to keep the talk in that vein. Hettner had come in for what he would call an intelligent and serious conversation; that is, he wanted to talk about himself, to give me hints as to what he really was, to tell me things about his soul. I could see that easily. Now, I do not want to know about people's souls; I want people quite entirely dressed; I want no display of fruity scabs and luscious sores. I like people's outsides, not their insides, and I was particularly reluctant to see this man's insides; they would be, probably, too much like mine.

He was talking in his quick, nervous, insolently humble voice, a voice without inflections that he poked at me, always stiffly, making his points with staccato rammings. The floor or the few lights in the dormitory across the field engaged most of his attention as he talked of philosophy and literature and history and music and art and all the bright niches he had chosen to hold that grubby little soul of his, but occasionally he jabbed his narrow eyes at me while he rammed me with his voice.

I poured him a second cup of tea and took down from the closet a bottle of gin.

"I bought this to see if I couldn't get inspiration for the writing of a story," I explained lightly, "but all I got was a thick head. I suppose if I can't seduce the Muse in the E. A. Poe style, I'll have to follow De Quincey and try opium. Though that sort of thing sounds more like rape than seduction."

He looked dubious as I held the square bottle over his cup. He probably never drank, but some idea of the "validity" of Dionysian frenzy kept him from refusing the pungent, colorless stream I let trickle into his tea.

"Sweeten it well. It makes a very nice drink."

He sat silent as he sampled the vitalized tea. He was wearing a blue serge suit, very shiny and worn, and a grimy tie. The suit was the only one he had, I knew, for he was poor, yet I very much resented it. Blue serge suits are all well enough, very handsome things, in fact, but when they are threadbare and lustrous they are detestable. A man may be as shabby as he pleases in a rough cloth, tweed or cheviot, and still look gay and interesting, but untidy blue serge gives him the look of a shop assistant.

Hettner looked at a picture on my wall, a soft lithograph framed in black, of a girl whose eyes were alight with a nervous energy and whose mouth lay in a soft repose. He had been talking about art, a subject on which he had done considerable reading and for which he had a timid scorn and mistrust. He asked me if the print was good. I told him that I did not know, that I usually judged a picture by the reputation of the artist and that I could not decipher the signature of this one; I guessed, however, that it was not very good, that the suggested shoulder was probably flagrantly misdrawn, but I explained why I liked it, for the eyes and the mouth, the thin nose and the lifted brows. He admitted that it was pretty and gazed at it for some time.

"If I knew a woman like that," he said very gravely, "I think I could . . ."

But I would not have him gravely conjecturing what would happen to him if he were to know a woman like that. For one thing, having once started on such a tack, I was not able to foretell how fatuously and to what length this lonely devil would discourse on love and sex and man and life. Besides, it was painful, even to me who did not like him, to imagine what the slender, volatile girl would do with his poor grubbiness. So I cut him off with, "No such luck, Hettner; all the pretty charming women are in the movies."

He ruminated for a moment. Then blankly, "The movies?" he repeated. The tea had been all consumed. He was holding his saucer and its empty cup in his bony hand. I reached for the gin and half filled the cup. He sipped it down and was silent for some time. . . .

He began now to talk about philosophy, about Dewey and the college infatuation with Santayana. The phrases that he poked at me with his hard unmodulated voice were good, biting phrases that somehow did not tell. He used a close, formal, literary turn of speech, unsoftened by idiom or colloquialism and he seldom had to search for a fugitive apt word. With a steady battering of talk he was trying to make a breach in my tower, to force for himself an opening through which he could reach in and snatch out my inter-est and sympathy, but I defended my citadel valiantly, almost en-joying the struggle, and when words did not serve me, I poured gin into his cup. He was always silent for a while after the consumption of the gin I had poured but it did not further affect him.

"I have been reading Spinoza a little," he said defiantly. I knew that he had not read a little, but most of Spinoza. He never was con-tent until he had read all that a man had written, every word. "What a superb and uncompromising mind! Blued steel—"

"Yes. He always was fascinating to me as the perfect example of the intellectual snobbery of the Jew."

He looked at the floor and was silent again. I had not intended it to be a thrust, but he seemed to take it so. He knew that he had been showing off intellectually at a frightful rate. When he spoke, it was more softly, with an attempt at casualness.

"I heard two men say last night that they were not afraid of death. They are, I suppose," and all the stiff irony played about his words again, "they are what is known as brave gentlemen, gallant soldiers in the battle of life. 'Life is not dancing but wrestling and one must learn to take one's falls gracefully, even the last.' Fah! The weak-kneed, well-bred asses! . . . Do you know it is said that at the moment before death the whole of a man's life comes rushing by, crowded and condensed into that one sick moment? To avoid that moment, if for no other reason, a man should fear to die."

It was a pretty idea and for a moment I toyed with it. Then, "Death," I said, "is life's best pal and severest critic," and I smiled.

The mouth that he kept in continual torture he had put on the rack again, and was stretching and twisting it until it seemed that it could no longer refrain from screaming its misery. His fingers were locked together, struggling. He wrenched them apart and reached suddenly for a cigarette. He lighted it and smoked for a few minutes. Then, with an agonized jerk, he got up from his chair and strolled around it once, stiffly. He dashed his cigarette furiously into the metal waste-basket and sat down, calmer.

"Don't you ever feel the pressure of the awful boredom that hangs over university life—if it is life? That endless, mild, eventless routine. If something would only happen, something new! But I suppose nothing *will* happen and there *is* nothing new under the sun."

"Nothing new under the sun—for the sun."

Across the field the lights of the dormitory had all gone out. Mine was perhaps the only window on the campus that was awake. The street cars had become so infrequent that now their rattling, when it came, was startling. The carts were coming down from the north of the city, the horses prodding each step precisely and unhurriedly, as though the drivers were dead and were being drawn in an endless funeral procession. Everything was quite dead and dark, except in my room where the cluster of three electric lights burned on the ceiling and Hettner and I engaged in battle, Hettner grave and purposeful, myself listening intently to what he had to say, polite and flippant. I sat on the table and Hettner on the chair, and he attacked and charged and I repelled and sallied. He understood that battle and its circumstances, and his efforts became frenzied, but now his understanding quite destroyed any hope of triumph. Earlier in the evening, if he had had the skill, he might have won through, but now it was impossible, and I, whose victories were few enough, smiled at that victory of mine.

The gin was gone and the night along with it. I sat on the table, on the half of the Browning paper I had written, and looked at Hettner. He was played out, exhausted as though after actual physical effort, but I was fresh and tremendously alive. We looked at each other for a long time. It was really rather funny, quite madly absurd, and I shuddered with the same exquisite sense of cruelty, sin and horror as when, a little boy, I held captive a blunt gray toad.

Hettner rose and stood at the door, his hand on the knob. There was a fine bitter light in his eyes. He turned to me and, not very loud, as though he were prefacing a long tirade that must begin low to reach its height of fury, said, "What a miserable dog you are."

I started. He was about to go on with what he had to say. Then he opened the door and ran down the corridor.

The Other Margaret

(From *Partisan Review*, 1945)

MARK JENNINGS stood the picture up on the wide counter and he and Stephen Elwin stepped back and looked at it. It was one of Rouault's kings. A person looking at it for the first time might find it repellent, even brutal or cruel. It was full of rude blacks that might seem barbarically untidy.

But the two men knew the picture well. They looked at it in silence. The admiration they were sharing made a community between them which at their age was rare, for they had both passed forty. Jennings waited for Elwin to speak first—they were friends but Elwin was the customer. Besides the frame had been designed by Jennings and in buying a reproduced picture the frame is of great importance, accounting for more than half the cost. Elwin had bought the picture some weeks before but he was seeing it framed for the first time.

Elwin said, "The frame is very good, Mark. It's perfect." He was a rather tall man with an attractive, competent face. He touched the frame curiously with the tip of his forefinger.

Jennings replied in a judicious tone, as if it were not his own good taste but that of a very gifted apprentice of his. "*I* think so," he said. And he too touched the frame, but intimately, rubbing briskly up and down one moulding with an artisan's possessive thumb, putting an unneeded last touch. He explained what considerations of color and proportion made the frame right for the picture. He spoke as if these were simple rules anyone might find in a book.

The king, blackbearded and crowned, faced in profile to the left. He had a fierce quality that had modulated, but not softened, to authority. One could feel of him—it was the reason why Elwin had bought the picture—that he had passed beyond ordinary matters of personality and was worthy of the crown he was wearing. Yet he was human and tragic. He was not unlike the sculptured kings of Chartres. In his right hand he held a spray of flowers.

"Is he a favorite of yours?" Elwin said. He did not know whether he meant the king or the king's painter. Indeed, as he asked the question, it seemed to him that he had assumed that the painter was this archaic personage himself. He had never imagined the painter painting the canvas with a brush. It was the beginning of a new thought about the picture.

Jennings answered with a modified version of the Latin gesture of esteem, a single decisive shake of his lifted hand, thumb and forefinger touching in a circle.

Elwin acknowledged the answer with a nod but said nothing. He did not want Jennings' admiration, even though he had asked for it. Jennings would naturally give as much admiration to most of the fine pictures in fine reproduction with which his shop was filled. At that moment, Elwin was not interested in admiration or in art. But he liked what Jennings said next.

"It will give you a lot of satisfaction," Jennings said. It was exactly as if he had just sold Elwin a suit or a pair of shoes.

Elwin said, "Yes," a little hesitatingly, only politely agreeing, not committing himself in the matter of his money's worth until it should be proved.

From behind the partition that made Jennings' little office they had been hearing a man talking on the telephone. Now the conversation ended and a young soldier, a second lieutenant, came out into the shop. Jennings said to him, "Did the call get through?" and the young man said, "Oh yes, after some difficulty. It was eighty-five cents. Let me pay you for it." "Oh nonsense," said Jennings, and took him by the arm and quickly introduced him to Elwin as a cousin of his wife's. The young man offered Elwin the hand that had been reaching into his pocket and said, "I'm glad to meet you, sir."

He said it very nicely, with the niceness that new young officers are likely to have. Pleased with themselves, they are certain that everyone will be nice to them. This young man's gold bar did a good deal for him, did perhaps more than rank ought to have to do for a man. He was not really much of a person. Yet Elwin, meeting him, felt the familiar emotion in which he could not distinguish guilt from envy. He knew it well, knew how to control it and it did not diminish, not much, the sense of holiday he was having. The holiday was made by his leaving his office a little early. He published scientific books in a small but successful way and the war had made a great pressure of work for him, but he had left his office early when Jennings phoned that the picture was back from the framer's.

The young lieutenant was looking at the picture. He so clearly did not like it that Jennings said quickly, "Mr. Elwin's just bought it."

The lieutenant regarded the picture thoughtfully. "Very nice," he said, with an enthusiastic and insincere shake of his head. He did not want to spoil things for Jennings by undermining the confidence of the customer. Elwin looked from the king to the lieutenant and back to the king. It was perfectly polite, only as if he had looked at the young man to hear his opinion more clearly and then had examined again the thing they were talking about.

But Jennings understood the movement of Elwin's glance, for

when the lieutenant had shaken hands and left the shop, Jennings
said stoutly, "He's a good kid."

"Yes, he is," Elwin said serenely.

"It's funny seeing him an officer. He used to be against anything
like that. But he was glad to go—he said he did not want to miss
sharing the experience of his generation."

"A lot of them say that." Elwin had heard it often from the
young men, the clever ones. Someone had started it and all the
young men with the semi-political views said it. Their reasons for
saying it were various. Elwin liked some of the reasons and disliked
others, but whether he liked the reasons or not, he never heard the
phrase without a twinge of envy. Now it comforted him to think
that this man with the black beard and the flower had done his
fighting without any remarks about experience and generations.

The idea of age and death did not present itself to Elwin in any
horrifying way. It had first come to him in the form of a sentence
from one of Hazlitt's essays. The sentence was, "No young man
believes he shall ever die," and the words had come to him suddenly
from the past, part of an elaborate recollection of a scene at high-
school. When he looked up the quotation, he found that he had
remembered it with perfect accuracy, down to that very *shall* which
struck his modern ear as odd and even ungrammatical. The memory had begun with the winter sunlight coming through the dirty
windows of the classroom. Then there was the color, texture and
smell of varnished wood. But these details were only pointing to the
teacher himself and what he was saying. He was a Mr. Baxter, a
heron-like man, esteemed as brilliant and eccentric, what some students called "a real person." Suddenly Mr. Baxter in a loud voice
had uttered that sentence of Hazlitt's. He held the book in his hand
but did not read from it. "No young man believes he shall ever die,"
he said, just as if he had thought of it himself.

It had been very startling to hear him say that, and this effect was of course just what the teacher wanted. It was the opening sentence of an essay called "On the Feeling of Immortality in Youth," and to Baxter it was important that the class should see what a bold and captivating way it was to begin an essay, how it was exactly as if someone had suddenly said the words, not written them after thought.

The chalky familiar classroom had been glorified by this moment of Mr. Baxter's. So many things had been said in the room, but here was one thing that had been said which was true. It was true in two ways. For Mr. Baxter it was true that no *young* man believes he shall ever die, but Mr. Baxter was not exactly a young man. For Stephen Elwin it was true that he would never die—he was scarcely even a young man yet, still only a boy. Between the student and the teacher the great difference was that the student would never die. Stephen Elwin had pitied Mr. Baxter and had been proud of himself. And mixed with the boy's feeling of immortality was a boy's pleasure at being involved with ideas which were not only solemn but complicated, for Mr. Baxter's mortality should have denied, but actually did not deny, the immortality that Stephen felt.

The Hazlitt sentence, once it had been remembered, had not left Elwin. Every now and then, sometimes just as he was falling asleep, sometimes just as he was waking up, sometimes right in the middle of anything at all, the sentence and the full awareness of what it meant would come to him. It felt like an internal explosion. It was not, however, an explosion of force but rather an explosion of light. It was not without pain but it was not wholly painful.

With the picture neatly wrapped in heavy brown paper, Elwin walked down Madison Avenue. It was still early. On a sudden impulse he walked west at 60th Street. Usually he came home by taxi, but this evening he thought of the Fifth Avenue bus, for some reason remembering that it was officially called a "coach" and that his father had spoken of it so, and had sometimes even referred to it as a "stage." The "coach" that he signaled was of the old kind, open wooden deck, platform at the rear, stairs connecting platform and deck with a big architectural curve. He saw it with surprise and affection. He had supposed that this model of bus had long been out of service and as he hailed it his mind sought for and found a word long unused. "DeDion," he said, pleased at having found it. "De-Dion Bouton."

He pronounced it *Deedeeon,* the way he and his friends had said it in 1917 when they had discussed the fine and powerful motors from Europe that were then being used for the buses. Some of them had been Fiats, but the most powerful of all were said to be the DeDions from France. No one knew the authority for this superlative judgment, but boys finding a pleasure in firm opinions did not care. Elwin remembered the special note in his friends' voices as they spoke of the DeDions. They talked about the great Mediterranean motors with a respect that was not only technical but historical. There had never been more than a few of the DeDions in America. Even in 1917 they were no longer being imported and the boys thought of them as old and rare.

Elwin took his seat inside the bus, at the rear. As suddenly as the name DeDion, it came to him how the open deck had once been a deck indeed—how, as sometimes the only passenger braving the weather up there, he had been the captain of the adventure, facing into the cold wind, even into the snow or rain, stoic, assailed but unmoved by the elements, inhaling health, fortitude and growth, for he had a boy's certainty that the more he endured, the stronger he would become. And when he had learned to board the bus and alight from it while it was still moving—"board" and "alight" were words the company used in its notices—how far advanced in life he had felt. So many landmarks of Elwin's boyhood in the city had vanished but this shabby bus had endured since the days when it had taken him daily to school.

At 82nd Street the bus stopped for a red light. A boy stood at the curb near the iron stanchion that bore the bus-stop sign. He clutched something in his hand. It must have been a coin, for he said to the conductor, "Mister, how much does it cost to ride on this bus?"

Elwin could not be sure of the boy's age, but he was perhaps twelve, Elwin's own age when he had been touched by his friends' elegiac discussions of the DeDions. The boy was not alone, he had a friend with him, and to see this friend, clearly a follower, was to understand the quality of the chief. The subaltern was a boy like any other, but the face of his leader was alight with the power of mind and a great urgency. Perhaps he was only late and in a hurry, but in any case the urgency illuminated his remarkable face.

The conductor did not answer the question.

"Mister," the boy said again, "how much does it cost to ride on this bus?"

His friend stood by, sharing passively in the question but saying nothing. They did not dare "board" until they knew whether or not their resources were sufficient.

The boy was dressed sturdily enough, perhaps for a boy of his age he was even well dressed. But he had been on the town or in the park most of the afternoon, or perhaps he had been one of those boys who, half in awe, half in rowdy levity, troop incessantly through the Egyptian rooms of the Museum, repeatedly entering and emerging from and entering again the narrow slits of the grave vaults. His knickerbockers were sliding at the knees and his effort to control a drop at his nose further compromised but by no mean destroyed his dignity. He had the clear cheeks and well-shaped head of a carefully reared child, but he seemed too far from home at this hour quite to be the child of very careful parents. There was an air about him which suggested that he had learned to expect at least a little resistance from the world and that he was ready to meet it.

The conductor did not reply to the second question. He had taken a large black wallet of imitation leather from some cranny of the rear platform and was making marks with a pencil on the cardboard trip-sheet it contained. He was an old man.

"Mister," said the boy again, and his voice, though tense, was reasonable. It was the very spirit of reasonableness. "Mister, how much does it cost to ride on this bus? A nickel or a dime?"

The conductor elaborately lifted his eyes from his record. He looked at the boy not hostilely nor yet quite facetiously, but with a certain quiet air of settled satisfaction. "What do you want to know for?" he said.

Elwin wanted to lower the window to tell the boy it was a dime. But he had waited too long. The conductor put his hand on the bell-button and gave the driver the signal. The light changed and the bus began to move.

"Mister!" the boy shouted. He may have been late to his supper but it was not this urgency that made his voice go up so loud and high. "For God's sake, mister!"

He of course did not bring in God by way of appeal. There was no longer any hope of his getting an answer. It was rather an expostulation with the unreasonable, the most passionate thing imaginable. Elwin looked back and saw the boy's hatred still following the conductor and, naturally, not only the conductor but the whole bus.

The conductor had now the modest look of a person who has just delivered a rebuke which was not only deserved but witty.

Well, Elwin thought, he is an old man and his pride is somewhere involved. Perhaps it was only that he could not at the moment bring himself to answer a question.

But he believed that in the past it could not have happened. When he was a boy the conductor might have said, "What do you want to know for?"—boys must always be teased a little by men. But the teasing would have stopped in time for him to board the bus. The bus was peculiarly safe. The people who rode in it and paid a dime after they had taken their seats were known to be nicer than the people who rode in the subway for a nickel which they paid before admission. It was the first public conveyance to which "nervous" parents entrusted their children—the conductors were known for their almost paternal kindness. For example, if you found on your trip to school that you had forgotten your money, the conductor would not fail to quiet the fear of authority that clutched your guilty heart. But this old man had outlived his fatherhood, which had once extended to all the bus-world of children. His own sons and daughters by now would have grown and gone and given him the usual causes for bitterness.

The old man's foolish triumph was something that must be understood. Elwin tried to know the weariness and sense of final loss that moved the old conductor to stand on that small dignity of his. He at once brought into consideration the conditions of life of the old man, especially the lack of all the advantages that he himself had had—the gentle rearing and the good education that made a man like Stephen Elwin answerable for all his actions. It had long been the habit of Elwin's mind to raise considerations of just this sort whenever he had reason to be annoyed with anyone who was not more powerful than himself.

But now, strangely, although the habit was in force, it did not check his anger. It was bewildering that he should feel anger at a poor ignorant man, a working man. It was the first time in his life that he had ever felt so. It shamed him. And he was the more bewildered and ashamed when he understood, as he did, that he was just as angry at the boy as at the old man. He was seeing the boy full grown and the self-pity and hatred taking root beside the urgency and power. The conductor and the boy were links in the great chain of the world's rage.

Clearly it was an unreasoning thing to feel. It was not what a wise man would feel. At this time in his life Stephen Elwin had the wish to be wise. He had never known a wise man. The very word sounded like something in a tale read to children. But the occasion for courage had passed. By courage Elwin meant something very simple, an unbending resistance of spirit under extreme physical difficulties. It was a boy's notion, but it had stayed with Elwin through most of his life, through his business and his pleasure, and nothing that he had ever done had given him the proof that he wanted. And now that the chance for that was gone—he was forty-one years old—it seemed to him that perhaps to be wise was almost as manly a thing as to be brave.

Two wars had passed Elwin by. For one he was too young, for the other too old, though by no means, of course, old. Had it not been for the war, and the consideration of age it so ruthlessly raised, the recollection of the sentence from Hazlitt would no doubt have been delayed by several years, and so too would the impulse to which it had given rise, the desire to have "wisdom." More and more in the last few months, Elwin had been able to experience the sensation of being wise, for it was indeed a sensation, a feeling of stamina, poise and illumination.

He was puzzled and unhappy as he "alighted" from the bus at 92nd Street. It seemed to him a great failure that his knowledge of death and his having reached the years of wisdom—they were the same thing—had not prevented him from feeling anger at an old man and a boy. It then occurred to him to think that perhaps he had felt his anger not in despite of wisdom but because of it. It was a disturbing, even a horrifying, fancy. Yet as he walked the two blocks to his home, he could not help recurring to it, with what was, as he had to see, a certain gratification.

In his pleasant living-room, in his comfortable chair, Stephen Elwin watched his daughter as she mixed the drink he usually had before dinner. She was thirteen. About a month ago she had made this her job, almost her duty, and she performed it with an unspeakable seriousness. She measured out the whiskey and poured it into the tumbler. With the ice-tongs she reached the ice gently into the bottom of the glass so that there would not be the least splash of whiskey. She opened the bottle of soda. Holding up the glass for her father's inspection, she poured the soda slowly, ready to stop at her father's word. Elwin cried "Whoa!" and at the word he thought that his daughter had reached the stage of her growth where she did indeed look like a well-bred pony.

Now Margaret was searching for the stirring-spoon. But she had forgotten to put it on the tray with all the other paraphernalia and she gave a little cry of vexation and went to fetch it. Elwin did not tell her not to bother, that it did not matter if the drink was not stirred. He understood that this business had to proceed with a ceremonial completeness.

Margaret returned with the stirring-spoon. She stirred the highball and the soda foamed up. She waited until it subsided, meanwhile shaking the spoon dry over the glass with three precise little shakes. She handed her father the drink and put a coaster on the table by his chair. She watched while he took his first sip. He had taken the whole responsibility for the proportion of soda to whiskey. Still, she wanted to be told that she had made the drink just right. Elwin said, "Fine. Just right," and Margaret tried not to show the absurd pleasure she felt.

For this ritual of Margaret's there were, as Elwin guessed, several motives. The honor of her home required that her father not make his own highball in the pantry and bring it out to drink in his chair, not after she had begun to take notice that in the homes of some of her schoolmates, every evening and not only at dinner-parties, a servant brought in, quite as a matter of course, a large tray of drinking equipment. But Margaret had other reasons than snobbishness—Elwin thought that she needed to establish a "custom," not only for now but for the future, against the time when she could say to her children, "And every night before dinner it was the *custom* in our family for me to make my father a drink." He supposed that this ritual of the drink was Margaret's first traffic with the future. It seemed to him that to know a thing like this about his daughter was one of the products of what could be called wisdom and he thought with irony but also with pleasure of his becoming a dim but necessary figure in Margaret's story of the past.

"I bought a picture today," Elwin said.

Margaret cocked an eye at him, as if to say, "Are you on the loose again?" She said, "What is it? Did you bring it home?"

"Oh, just a reproduction, a Rouault."

"Rouault?" she said. She shook her head decisively. "Don't know him." It quite settled Rouault for the moment.

"Don't know him?"

"Never heard of him."

"Well, take a look at it—it's over there."

She untied the string and took off the paper and sat there on the big hassock, her feet far out in front of her, holding the great king at arm's length. It was to Elwin strange and funny, this confrontation of the black, calm, tragic king and this blonde child in her sweater and skirt, in her moccasin shoes. She became abstracted and withdrawn in her scrutiny of the picture. Then Elwin, seeing the breadth and brightness of her brow, the steady intelligence of her gaze, understood that there was really no comic disproportion. What was funny was the equality. The young lieutenant had been quite neutralized by the picture. Even Mark Jennings had been a little diminished by it. But Margaret, with her grave, luminous brow, was able to meet it head on. And not in agreement either.

"You don't like it?" Elwin said.

She looked from the picture to him and said, "I don't think so."

She said it softly but it was pretty positive. She herself painted and she was in a very simple relation to pictures. She rose and placed the picture on the sofa as if to give it another chance in a different position and a better light. She stood at a distance and looked at it and Elwin stood behind her to get the same view of it that she had. He put his hand on her shoulder. After a moment she looked up at him and smiled. "I don't really *like* it," she said. The modulation of her voice was not apology, but simply a gesture of making room for another opinion. She did not think it was important whether she liked or disliked the picture. It said something to her that was not in her experience or that she did not want in her experience. Liking the picture would have given her pleasure. She got no pleasure from not liking it. It seemed to Elwin that in the little shake of her head, in her tone and smile, there was a quality, really monumental, by which he could explain his anger at the old conductor and the boy and forgive himself for having had it.

When Lucy Elwin came in, her face was flushed from the stove and she had a look of triumphant anticipation. She shamelessly communicated this to her family. "It's going to be ve-ry good," she said, not as if she were promising them a fine dinner, rather as if she were threatening them with a grim fate. She meant that her dinner was going to be so very good that if they did not extravagantly admire it, if they merely took it for granted, they would be made to feel sorry. "It will be ready in about ten minutes," she said. "Are you very hungry?"

"Just enough," Elwin said. "Are you tired?" For his wife had stretched out in the armchair and put back her head. She slouched with her long legs at full length, her skirt a little disordered, one ankle laid on the other. Her eyes being closed made her complicated face look simple and she seemed young and self-indulgent, like a girl who escapes from the embarrassment of herself into a broody trance. It was an attitude that had lately become frequent with Margaret.

Lucy Elwin said, "Yes, a little tired. But really, you know, I'd almost rather do the work myself than have that Margaret around."

She spoke with her eyes still closed, and so she did not see her daughter stiffen. But Elwin did. He knew that it was not because Margaret thought that her mother meant her but because of the feelings she had for the other Margaret, the maid. The other Margaret, as so often, had not come to work that day.

Margaret had mixed a drink for her mother and now she was standing beside Lucy's chair, waiting with exaggerated patience for Lucy to open her eyes. She said, "Here's your drink, mother!"

She said it as if she had waited quite long enough, using the lumpish, martyred, unsuccessful irony of thirteen, her eyebrows very weary, the expression of her mouth very dry. Lucy opened her eyes and sat up straight in her chair. She took the drink from Margaret and smiled. "Thank you, dear," she said. For the moment it was as if Margaret were the mother, full of rectitude and manners, and Lucy the careless daughter.

That Lucy was being careless even her husband felt. No one could say of their Negro maid, the other Margaret, that she was a pleasant person. Even Elwin would have to admit to a sense of strain in her presence. But surely Lucy took too passionate a notice of her. Elwin felt that this was not in keeping with his wife's nature. But no, that was really not so. It was often disquieting to Elwin, the willingness that Lucy had to get angry even with simple people when she thought they were not behaving well. And lately she had been full of stories about the nasty and insulted temper that was being shown by the people one daily dealt with. Only yesterday, for example, there had been her story of the soda-fountain man who made a point of mopping and puttering and changing the position of pieces of pie and only after he had shown his indifference and independence would take your order. Elwin had to balance against the notice his wife took of such things the deep, literal, almost childish way she spoke of them, the innocence of her passion. But this particular story of the soda-fountain clerk had really distressed him, actually embarrassing him for Lucy, and he had pointed out to her how frequent such stories had become. She had simply stared at him, the fact was so very clear. "Why, it's the war," she said. "People are just much meaner since the war." And when his rebuke had moved on to the matter of the maid Margaret, Lucy had said in the most matter-of-fact way, "Why, she just hates us." And she had shocked

Elwin by giving, just like any middle-class housewife, a list of all the precious things Margaret had broken. "And observe," Lucy had said, "that never once has she broken anything cheap or ordinary, only the things I've pointed out to her that needed care."

Elwin had to admit that the list made a case. Still, even if the number of the green Wedgwood coffee cups had been much diminished, cups for which Elwin himself had a special fondness, and even if the Persian bowl had been dropped and the glass urn they had brought from Sweden had been cracked in the sink, they must surely not talk of such things. The very costliness of the objects which proved Margaret's animosity, the very affection which the Elwins felt for them, made the whole situation impossible to consider.

Lucy must indeed have been unaware of how deeply her husband resisted her carelessness in these matters and of what her daughter was now feeling. Otherwise she would not have begun her story, her eyes narrowing in anger at the recollection, "Oh, such a rotten thing happened on the way home on the bus."

It was Elwin who had had the thing happen on the bus, not quite "rotten" but sufficiently disturbing, and he was startled, as if his wife's consciousness had in some way become mixed up with his own in a clairvoyant experience. And this feeling was not diminished as Lucy told her story about a young woman who had asked the conductor a question. It was a simple, ordinary question Lucy said, about what street one transferred at. The conductor at first had not answered, and then, when he came around again and the question was asked again, he had looked at the young woman—"looked her straight in the face," Lucy said—and had replied in a loud voice, "Vot deed you shay?"

"Mother!" cried Margaret. Her voice was all absolute childish horror.

Elwin at once saw what was happening, but Lucy, absorbed in what she had experienced, only said mildly, "What's the matter, dear?"

"Mother!" Margaret grieved, "you mustn't do that." Her face was quite aghast and she was standing stiff with actual fright.

"Why, do what, Margaret?" said Lucy. She was troubled for her daughter but entirely bewildered.

"Make fun of—fun of—" But Margaret could not say it.

"Of Jews?" said Elwin in a loud, firm, downright voice.

Margaret nodded miserably. Elwin said with enough sharpness, "Margaret, whatever makes you think that Lucy is making fun of Jews? She is simply repeating—"

"Oh," Margaret cried, her face a silly little moon of gratitude and relief. "Oh," she said happily. "What the woman said to the conductor!"

"No, Margaret. How absurd!" Lucy cried. "*Not* what the woman said to the conductor. What the conductor said to the woman."

Margaret just sat there glowering with silence and anger.

Elwin said to Margaret with a pedagogic clearness and patience, "The conductor was making fun of the woman for being Jewish."

"Not at all," Lucy said, beginning to be a little tried by so much misunderstanding. "Not at all, she wasn't Jewish at all. He was insulting her by pretending that she was Jewish."

Margaret had only one question to ask. "The *conductor?*" she cried with desperate emphasis.

And when Lucy said that it was indeed the conductor, Margaret said nothing, but shrugged her shoulders in an elaborate way and made with her hands a large grimace of despairing incomprehension. She was dismissing the grownups by this pantomime, appealing beyond all their sad nonsense to her own world of sure right reason. In that world one knew where one was, one knew that to say things about Jews was bad and that working men were good. And *therefore*.

Elwin, whose awareness was all aroused, wondered in tender amusement what his daughter would have felt if she had known that her gesture, which she had drawn from the large available stock of the folk-culture of children, had originally been a satiric mimicry of a puzzled shrugging Jew. The Margaret who stood there in sullenness was so very different from the Margaret who, only a few minutes before, had looked at the picture with him and had seemed, almost, to be teaching him something. Now he had to teach her. "That isn't a very pretty gesture," he said. "And what, please, is so difficult about Lucy's story? Don't you believe it?"

A mistake, as he saw at once. Margaret was standing there trapped —no, she did not believe it, but she did not dare say so. Elwin corrected himself and gave her her chance. "Do you think Lucy didn't hear right?"

Margaret nodded eagerly, humbly glad to take the way out that was being offered her.

"We studied the transit system," she said by way of explanation. "We made a study of it." She stopped. Elwin knew how her argument ran, but she herself was not entirely sure of it. She said tentatively, by way of a beginning, "They are underpaid."

Lucy was being really irresponsible, Elwin thought, for she said in an abstracted tone, as if she were musing on the early clues of an interesting scientific generalization, "They hate *women*—it's women they're always rude to. Never the men." Margaret's face flushed, and her eyes darkened at this new expression of her mother's moral obtuseness, and Elwin felt a quick impatience with his daughter's sensitivity—it seemed suddenly to have taken on a pedantic air. But he was annoyed with Lucy too, who ought surely be more aware of what her daughter was feeling. No doubt he was the more annoyed because his own incident of the bus was untold and would remain untold. But it was Lucy who saved the situation she had created. She suddenly remembered the kitchen. She hurried out, then came back, caught Margaret by the arm in a bustle of haste and said, "Come and hurl the salad." This was a famous new joke in the family. Elwin had made it, Margaret loved it. It had reference to a "tossed green salad" on a pretentious restaurant menu. Of the salad, when it was served to them in all its wiltedness, Elwin had said that apparently it needed to be more than tossed, it needed to be hurled.

And so all at once the family was restored, a family with a family joke. Margaret stood there grinning in the embarrassment of the voluptuous pleasure she felt at happiness returned. But she must have been very angry with her mother, for she came back and pulled Elwin's head down and whispered into his ear where he would be able to find and inspect the presents she had for Lucy's birthday next week.

He was to look for two things. In the top left-hand drawer of Margaret's desk he would find the "bought present" and on the shelf in the clothes closet he would find the "made present." The bought present was a wallet, a beautiful green wallet, so clearly expensive that Elwin understood why his daughter had had to tease him for money to supplement her savings, and so adult in its expensiveness that he had to understand how inexorably she was growing up.

The made present was also green, a green lamb, large enough to have to be held in two hands, with black feet and wide black eyes. The eyes stared out with a great charming question to the world, expressing the comic grace of the lamb's awkwardness. Elwin wondered if Margaret had been at all aware of how much the lamb was a self-portrait. When Elwin, some two years before, had listened to his daughter playing her first full piece on the recorder, he had thought that nothing could be more wonderful than the impervious gravity of her face as her eyes focussed on the bell of the instrument and on the music-book while she blew her tune in a daze of concentration; yet only a few months later, when she had progressed so far as to be up to airs from Mozart, she had been able, in the very midst of a roulade, with her fingers moving fast, to glance up at him with a twinkling, sidelong look, her mouth puckering in a smile as she kept her lips pursed, amused by the music, amused by the frank excess of its ornamentation and by her own virtuosity. For Elwin

the smile was the expression of gay and conscious life, of life inno-
cently aware of itself and fond of itself, and, although there was
something painful in having to make the admission, it was even
more endearing than Margaret's earlier gravity. Life aware of itself
seemed so much more life.

His daughter's room was full of life. His own old microscope
stood on Margaret's desk and around it was a litter of slides and of
the various objects from which she had been cutting sections, a
prune and a dried apricot, a sliver of wood, a piece of cheese and what
seemed to be a cockroach. There were tools for carving wood and
for cutting linoleum blocks. The books were beginning to be too
many for the small bookshelf, starting with *The Little Family* and
going on to his own soiled copy of *The Light That Failed* that Margaret had unearthed. There was her easel and on one wall was a
print of Picasso's trapeze people in flight, like fierce flames, and on
another wall one of Benton's righteous stylizations, both at home,
knowing nothing of their antagonism to each other. The dolls were
no longer so much to the fore as they once were, but they were still
about, and so was the elaborate doll's house which contained in precise miniature, accumulated over years, almost every object of daily
living, tiny skillets, lamps, cups, kettles, packaged groceries. Sur-
rounded by all that his daughter made and did and read, Elwin
could not understand how she found the time. And then, on the
thought of what time could be to a child, there came to him with
more painful illumination than usual, the recurrent sentence, "No
young man believes he shall ever die." And he stood contemplating
the room with a kind of desolation of love for it.

Margaret burst in suddenly as if she were running away from
something—as indeed she was, for her eyes blazed with the anger
she was fleeing. She flung herself on the bed, ignoring her father's
presence.

"Margaret, what's the matter?" Elwin said.

But she did not answer.

"Margaret!" There was the note of discipline in his voice. "Tell me what the matter is."

She was not crying, but her face, when she lifted it from the pillow, was red and swollen. "It's mother," she said. "The way she talked to Margaret."

"To Margaret? Has Margaret come?"

"Yes, she came." The tone implied: through flood and fire. "And mother—oh!" She broke off and shook her head in a rather histrionic expression of how impossible it was to tell what her mother had done.

"What did she say that was so terrible?"

"She said—she said, 'Look here—'" But Margaret could not go on.

Lucy strode into the room with quite as much impulse as Margaret had and with eyes blazing as fiercely as her daughter's. "Look here, Margaret," she said. "I've quite enough trouble with that Margaret without your nonsense. Nobody is being exploited in this house and nobody is being bullied and I'm not going to have you making situations about nothing. I'm sure your Miss Hoxie is very sweet and nice, but you seem to have got your ideas from her all mixed up. You weren't that way about Millie when she was with us. As a matter of fact," Lucy said with remorseless irony, "you were often not at all nice to her."

Margaret had not heard the end of Lucy's speech. At the mention of Miss Hoxie in the tone that Lucy had used—"your Miss Hoxie" —at the sacred name of her teacher blasphemously uttered, she looked at her mother with the horror of seeing her now in her true terrible colors. The last bond between them had snapped at this attack upon her heart's best loyalty.

But Lucy was taking no account of finer feelings. She closed the door and said firmly, "Now look here, the simple fact is that that Margaret is a thoroughly disagreeable person, a nasty, mean person."

"Oh, she is not," Margaret wailed. And then, despite all her passion, the simple fact broke in upon her irresistibly. Elwin's heart quite melted as he saw her confront the fact and struggle with it. For the fact was as Lucy had stated it, and he himself at that moment had to realize it. And it was wonderful to see that Margaret's mind, whatever the inclination of her will, was unable to resist a fact. But the mind that had momentarily deserted her will, came quickly again to its help. "She's not responsible," she said desperately. "It's not her fault. She couldn't help it. Society—" But at that big word she halted, unable to handle it. "We can't blame her," she said defiantly but a little lamely.

At that moment Lucy saw the green clay lamb that Elwin was still holding. She rushed to it and took it and cried, "Margaret, is this yours? I've never seen it, why didn't you show it to me?"

It was, of course, a decided point for Margaret that her birthday surprise was spoiled. She sat there looking dry and indifferent amid the ruins of family custom. Elwin said, "It's a birthday present for you, Lucy. You weren't supposed to see it," and their glances met briefly. He had been a little treacherous, for he could have managed to put the lamb out of sight, but some craftiness, not entirely conscious, had suggested its usefulness for peace.

"It's so *lovely*," Lucy said. "Is it really for me?"

Margaret had to acknowledge that it was, but with an elaborate ungraciousness from her bruised and empty heart. Her mother might have the gift, meaningless as it now was. But Lucy was in a flood of thanks and praise impossible to withstand—it was lovely, she said, to have a gift in advance of her birthday, it was something she had always wanted as a child and had never been able to induce her parents to allow, that she should have one, just one, of her presents before the others, and the lamb itself was simply beautiful, quite the nicest thing Margaret had ever made. "Oh, I love it," she said, stroking its face and then its rump. "Why darling!" she cried, "it looks exactly like you!" And Margaret had to submit to the child's pain at seeing the eminence of grief and grievance swept away. But at last, carried beyond the vacant moment when the forgiving and forgiven feeling had not yet come, she sat there in an embarrassed glow, beaming shyly as her mother kissed her and said quietly and finally, "Thank you."

When they were in the dining-room, all three of them feeling chastened and purged, Lucy said, "I must have it here by my place." And she put the lamb by her at the table, touching its cheek affectionately.

The dinner that Lucy had cooked was served by the other Margaret. She was a tall, rather light-colored girl, with a genteel manner and eyebrows that were now kept very high. As she presented the casserole to Lucy, she looked far off into a distance and stood a little too far away for convenience. Lucy sat there with the serving spoon and fork in her hand and then said, "Come a little closer, Margaret." Margaret Elwin sat rigid, watching. Margaret the maid edged a little closer and continued her gaze. She moved to serve Elwin but Lucy said, "It's Margaret you serve next." Her tone was a little dry. Margaret Elwin flushed and looked mortified. It had been a matter of some satisfaction that she was now of an age to be served at table just after her mother, but she hated to have a point made of it if Margaret objected, and Margaret did seem to object and would not accept the reassuring smile that was being offered her over the casserole.

In the interval between the serving of the casserole and the serving of the salad that had once that evening made the family peace, Margaret held her parents with a stern and desperate eye. But she was unable to suppress a glance her mother sent to her father, a glance that had in it a touch of mild triumph. And her father did not this time fortify himself against it. The odds were terribly against her and she looked from one to the other and said in an intense whisper, "It's not her fault. She's not responsible."

"Why not?" Elwin asked.

It was his voice that made the question baffling to Margaret. She did not answer, or try to. It was not merely that the question was, for the moment, beyond her powers. Nor was it that she was puzzled because her father had seemed to change sides. But she was touched by the sense, so little formulated, so fleeting as scarcely to establish itself in her memory, that something other than the question, or the problem itself, was involved here. She barely perceived, yet she did perceive, her mother's quick glance at her father under lowered lids. It was something more than a glance of surprise. Neither Margaret nor Lucy, of course, knew anything about the sentence from Hazlitt. But this was one of the moments when the sentence had occurred to Elwin and with it the explosion of light. And his wife and daughter had heard the event in his voice. For Elwin an illumination, but a dark illumination, was thrown around the matter that concerned them. It seemed to him—not suddenly, for it had been advancing in his mind for some hours now—that in the aspect of his knowledge of death, all men were equal in their responsibility. The two bus conductors, Lucy's and his own, the boy with his face contorted in rational rage against the injustice he suffered, Margaret the maid with her genteel malice—all of them, quite as much as he himself, bore their own blame. Exemption was not given by age or youth, or sex, or color, or condition of life. It was the sense of this that made his voice so strange at his own dinner-table, as if it came not merely from another place but another time.

"Why not?" he said again. "Why not, Margaret?"

Margaret looked at her father's face and tried to answer. She seriously marshalled her thoughts and, as always, the sight of his daughter actually thinking touched Elwin profoundly. "It's because—because society didn't give her a chance," she said slowly. "She has a handicap. Because she's colored. She has to struggle so hard—against prejudice. It's so *hard* for her."

"It's true," Elwin said. "It's very hard for her. But it's hard for Millie too." Millie had been with the Elwins for nearly seven years. Some months ago she had left them to nurse a dying sister in the South.

Margaret of course knew what her father meant, that Millie, despite "society," was warm and good and capable. Her answer was quick, too quick. "Oh, Millie has a slave-psychology," she said loftily.

Really, Elwin thought, Miss Hoxie went too far. He felt a kind of disgust that a child should have been given such a phrase to use. It was a good school, he approved of its theory; but it must not give Margaret such things to say. He wondered if Margaret had submitted the question of Millie to Miss Hoxie. If she had, and if this was the answer she had been given, his daughter had been, yes, corrupted. He said, "You should not say such things about Millie. She is a good loyal person and you haven't any right to say she is not."

"Loyal!" said Margaret in triumph. "Loyal."

"Why yes. To her sister in Alabama, Margaret, just as much as to us. Is it what you call slave-psychology to be loyal to your own sister?"

But Margaret was not to be put down. She kept in mind the main point, which was not Millie but the other Margaret.

"I notice," she said defiantly, "that when Millie sends you parts of the money you lent her, you take it all right."

Poor child, she had fumbled, and Elwin laid his hand on hers on the table. "But Margaret! Of course I do," he said. "If I didn't, wouldn't that be slave-psychology? Millie would feel very lowered if I didn't take it."

"But she can't afford it," Margaret insisted.

"No, she can't afford it."

"Well then!" and she confronted the oppressor in her father.

"But she can't afford not to. She needs it for her pride. She needs to think of herself as a person who pays her debts, as a responsible person."

"I wonder," Lucy said, "I wonder how Millie is. Poor thing!" She was not being irrelevant. She was successful in bringing her husband up short. Yes, all that his "wisdom" had done was to lead him to defeat his daughter in argument. And defeat made Margaret stupid and obstinate. She said, "Well, anyway, it's not Margaret's fault," and sat sulking.

Had he been truly the wise man he wanted to be, he would have been able to explain, to Margaret and himself, the nature of the double truth. As much as Margaret, he believed that "society is responsible." He believed the other truth too. He felt rather tired, as if the little debate with Margaret had been more momentous than he understood. Yet wisdom, a small measure of it, did seem to come. It came suddenly, as no doubt was the way of moments of wisdom, and he perceived what stupidly he had not understood earlier, that it was not the other Margaret but herself that his Margaret was grieving for, that in her foolish and passionate argument, with the foolish phrases derived from the admired Miss Hoxie, she was defending herself from her own impending responsibility. Poor thing, she saw it moving toward her through the air at a great rate, and she did not want it. Naturally enough, she did not want it. And he, for what reason he did not know, was forcing it upon her.

He understood why Lucy, when they had risen from the table, made quiet haste to put her arm around Margaret's shoulders as they went into the living-room.

They were sitting in the living-room, a rather silent family for the moment, when the other Margaret stood in the doorway. "You may as well know," she said, "that I'm through here." And she added, "I've had enough."

There was a little cry, as of horror, from Margaret. She looked at her parents with a bitter and tragic triumph. Lucy said shortly, "Very well, Margaret. Just finish up and I'll pay you." The quick acceptance took the maid aback. Angrier than before, she turned abruptly back into the dining-room.

For the third time that evening, Margaret Elwin sat in wretched isolation. Her father did not watch her, but he knew what she felt. She had been told *she* might go, never to return. She saw the great and frightening world before her. It was after all possible so to offend her parents that this expulsion would follow. Elwin rose to get a cigarette from the table near the sofa on which Margaret sat and he passed his hand over her bright hair. The picture of the king with the flower in his hand was in the other corner of the sofa.

It was as Elwin's hand was on his daughter's head that they heard the crash, and Elwin felt under his hand how Margaret's body experienced a kind of convulsion. He turned and saw Lucy already at the door of the dining-room, while there on the floor, in many pieces, as if it had fallen with force, lay the smashed green lamb, more white clay showing than green glaze. Lucy stooped down to the fragments, examining them, delicately turning them over one by one, as if already estimating the possibility of mending.

The maid Margaret stood there, a napkin in her hand clutched to her breast. All the genteel contempt had left her face. She looked only frightened, as if something was now, at last, going to be done to her. For her, almost more than for his own Margaret, Elwin felt sad. He said, "It's all right, Margaret. Don't worry, it's all right." It was a foolish and weak thing to say. It was not all right, and Lucy was still crouching, heartbroken, over the pieces. But he had had to say it, weak and foolish as it was.

"Ah, darling, don't feel too bad," Lucy said to her daughter as she came back into the living-room, tenderly holding the smashed thing in her hand.

But Margaret did not answer or even hear. She was staring into the dining-room with wide, fixed eyes. "She meant to do it," she said. "She *meant* to do it."

"Oh, no," Lucy said in her most matter-of-fact voice. "Oh, no, dear. It was just an accident."

"She meant to do it, she meant to do it." And then Margaret said, "I *saw* her." She alone had been facing into the dining-room and could have seen. "I saw her—with the napkin. She made a movement," and Margaret made a movement, "like this . . ."

Over her head her parents' eyes met. They knew that they could only offer the feeble lying of parents to a child. But they were determined to continue. "Oh, no," Elwin said, "it just happened." And he wondered if the king, within his line of vision as he stood there trying to comfort his daughter, would ever return to the old, fine, tragic power, for at the moment he seemed only quaint, extravagant and beside the point.

"She meant to. She didn't like me. She hated me," and the great sobs began to come. But Elwin knew that it was not because the other Margaret hated her that his Margaret wept, but because she had with her own eyes seen the actual possibility of what she herself might do, the insupportable fact of her own moral life. She was weeping bitterly now, her whole body shaking with the deepest of sobs, and she found refuge in a corner of the sofa, hiding her head from her parents. She had drawn up her knees, making herself as tight and inaccessible as she could, and Elwin, to comfort her, sat on what little space she allowed him on the sofa beside her, stroking her burrowing head and her heaving back, quite unable, whatever he might have hoped and wanted, to give her any better help than that.

Notes on a Departure

(From *The Menorah Journal*, 1929)

I travel on by barren farms,
And gulls glint out like silver flecks
Against a cloud that speaks of wrecks,
And bellies down with black alarms.
I say: "Thus from my lady's arms
I go; those arms I love the best!"
The wind replies from dip and rise,
"Nay; toward her arms thou journeyest."
—THOMAS HARDY

I

HE saw from the way his visitor was slowly drawing in his long legs with careful and polite unconcern that the boy thought it time to go. He therefore made his own talk tentative and intermittent so that the visit could be terminated with ease and unabruptness. He did not want the visit to end quite yet, not that he had anything more to say, and he did not want the boy to think that he was being dismissed. But the boy rose and stepped over a corded box of books to the door.

"So you won't be back again next year, sir? I'll bet you're guh-glad. Maybe I won't be either if my muh-marks are what I expect." The boy smiled with pride on his own scholastic laxness.

"I thought you did good work, McAllister. Your English was certainly good." The teacher, proud of his student, smiled to him to show his amused pride.

"No. English was my best cuh-cuh-course. I'll be lucky if I only flunk one." The boy had a stammer that caught a word in every sentence.

"Too bad. Well . . ." said the teacher, and then, with an affectedly judicious meditation, "No, I don't think I shall be very glad. Oh, a little, it's been dull sometimes, but I've enjoyed it. No; not altogether glad."

Indeed, he was sorry that he would never see this boy again, and for a moment he felt for him, leaning against the door-jamb and standing almost as tall as it, a deep and simple affection. He felt short and broad, very old, very wise, very empty, beside this superb height. He wanted to do something protective and paternal for the boy, and smiled to think that there was scarcely a disparity of two years in their ages. Checking the utterance of a request that the boy write him, for it would only seem a conventional gesture and its fulfilment could only be irksome and disappointing, he held out his hand.

"Good-bye, McAllister. It's been nice to have known you and had you in the class."

"Good-bye, sir. I liked it a huh-hell of a lot. Good luck."

"Good luck to *you,* McAllister. I'll be looking out to see your name in print."

"Thank you. I hope so. Good-bye."

"Good-bye."

He watched the tall, fine figure walk down the dusky corridor, the blond head brightening rhythmically as it encountered and passed through the broad, sharp-edged beams of morning sunlight that came through the glass panels of the doors. Old, wise and empty: he felt that he was being made ridiculous and anomalous, and he turned back into the dismantled room, trying to suppress the feeling of unreal frustration which had come from this emotion he did not know what to do with.

———

In a strange and hidden but quite real way, McAllister had played an important part in this past year of his. A tall, handsome boy, who spoke with a sweet, unconscious courtesy and a nursery stammer; whose face, though firmly molded and even marked into lines of wisdom and strength, was yet puerilely irrelevant to life; whose eyes looked out into an undiscoverable distance; and whose mouth was formed to say some such quietly melodramatic thing as, "There is no return. Forward. March forward," McAllister never became a person, but was always some yellow-haired, graceful materialization of story. He came to call and was graciously deferential telling about his life, but he lived in a world that surely he must spin out of himself, that surely did not exist. Most certainly McAllister was not a person. And because the teacher felt that he himself was a person or that it was his duty to become one, there grew up between teacher and student a shyness that was not hostile but which was, indeed, rather a friendly salute.

The teacher had said to his classes, "Now, in writing these autobiographies, please do not try to startle me. Don't try to fabricate a romance. I don't expect you to have had your true-loves die in your arms, nor that you fought a duel at twelve paces. But little things have happened to all of us which in a way are just as important: how the wind felt the day we ran away from home, the smell of apples in the cellar. These are not always very dramatic, but they are interesting and important. Write about these things. . . . For Monday, then, I want a tentative outline of your autobiographies." So all had outlined the commonplaces of existence. But McAllister had been a bouncer in a brothel-cabaret, a circus tumbler, a professional boxer and a stunt aviator, one of those men who jump from the landing gear of a machine in flight to the wings of another below. He had sat all the term, very correctly dressed, very unconscious of the covert stares of the girls, dull, handsome, conventional.

They came to know each other better after McAllister brought around for inspection a load of bad poems and some startlingly effective, if tawdry, prose. His father had been a boxer who had studied dentistry and had become a professor in a dental college. He adored his father, who had been able to read Persian and who was now dead. His mother, whom he called, quite seriously, "a gracious Presbyterian gentlewoman," he tolerated amusedly. He had a broken rib which could not be mended. If he were hit hard there he would be gone, for the rib was within an inch of his heart and if it touched the heart, well, good-night, he popped off.

"You got it broken after you were a boxer?"

"No, before—in football."

"Before? But suppose you got hit there?"

"There's not much chance. You see, if you keep your guard up properly," he demonstrated, "they can't touch you there."

He idled through the terms, writing mad themes about a world which he had picked up somewhere, of "bitterness," "courage," "defeat," "glorious adventure," "ironic perversity." He said things that are silly. "I want my life to be short and intense. I want to die in action. I am glad of my busted rib, it's a sort of talisman to me." "Sin is like stunt flying. It's dangerous, but it gets dull anyway." But they did not sound completely silly.

And the town had been like McAllister. It had deceived by an appearance of simple dullness. Then, little by little, he had seen it open itself and it had not been dull. And neither was it real. (How to prove judgments of reality he did not know, but that such judgments could be made he was sure. Some things were not real, even though one could talk of them confidently, touch them, live with and by them.) But where McAllister's unreality had generated a shyness, the town, stronger than McAllister, had generated by its unreality a stronger emotion, fear. It, too, like McAllister, often said silly things; but somehow it, too, made him feel that they were not completely silly—because, he supposed, like the silly things Mc-Allister said, they had the power to make him feel old, wise and empty.

Too often the town had made him feel as he had felt when his contemporaries in the department had been in the very thick of admiration for de Gourmont and he, amazed at their rhapsodies, had looked again into *A Night in the Luxembourg*. He had sat puzzled and hurt before it. All the graceful, intelligent fleshliness had meant nothing. Far from being scornful, he had felt a jealousy. It was the gnawing jealousy, which is dismissed quickly but which recurs, which old age has of the youth around it. The town knew that he was young but it had decided, it seemed, that he had the wizened face which is commonly supposed to belong to youthful musical or chess prodigies and which youthful dress but makes the more decrepit. The town approached him with a kind of contemptuous awe for the acceleration of his years. And he had succumbed to the town's force; a heavy senility seemed to touch him lightly all over. . . .

Now the town lay beautifully quiet, and for the past few weeks it had gone into a sunlit stillness. It had been lying hushed and quiet; the blue lake lay at its feet, noisy and tumultuous in crude spring, now broad-bosomed and soft in early summer; wide winds moved in softly from the lake and passed through the streets overarched with interlocking elms, their leaves already warm and dusty. The cool mornings touched one at every point with clarity; the afternoons were great and ripe; the twilights had a trick of hanging long and they deepened into velvety nights with autumnal orange moons. The students moved with a new grace among the trees and along streets; their movements expressed the almost conscious arrogance of their youth. Some evenings, tall girls in dance dresses that were short-skirted in front and drooped long and heavily in back stood on the fraternity docks and looked out over the lake with their escorts and rested from dancing. He wandered about and allowed the access of an elegant pain: it was an emotion that had been dealt with almost exclusively by bad writers, but he allowed it.

Intimacies sprang up. He met men casually and walked lengthily with them. People dropped lazily in upon him, lounged on his bed, dabbled in talk, borrowed something, and left easily. He visited and went to parties. No longer did he look with worried eyes at what the town might do to him, nor did he feel that each gesture of comfort and friendliness was a self-betrayal. It was pleasant and he felt "at home"—not quite "at home," for he had just enough strangeness to be conscious of the feeling, to enjoy it.

But he did not forget that, before he had been able to accept the town with the lightness he now used, he had first had to destroy it and make it as nothing. Once he had felt that the town was going to make him do things he must not do. It sought to include him in a life into which he must not go. To prevent this he had made use of a hitherto useless fact. He had said, "I am a Jew," and immediately he was free. He had felt himself the embodiment of an antique and separate race—and consecrated? he had asked himself with a snicker —and was made unable to partake of what he thought the danger that lay in town and university. He had made a companion of the solitude he had gained, gazed fondly and admiringly at it; he had made an exorcising charm of it and when he touched it the town became harmless.

But if he embodied the separateness of his race, a good thing, he found, too, that he had assumed its antiquity. Perhaps the town, recognizing what he had done, had said, "If you will be as apart as a Jew, be also as old as a Jew," and he had obeyed.

With McAllister, his decrepitude was sharp and intense and therefore a little controllable. But with the town and the university, the intimidation into senescence was diffused and vague; it hung about him in a cloud which, when his mind struck into it, was unaffected.

Upon McAllister was set the sweet sign of eternal youth. And upon the town the same sign was also set. McAllister, he had perceived at the beginning, would never change. And the town, with the stream of youth constantly flowing into it, keeping everything young, would never change. And he was very old.

Yet early in his acquaintance with the town, even before he had been intimidated into age, he thought he perceived in it, despite its youth, a spot of death. The town, he learned to see, would ever gyrate in an unceasing vortex of youth. (He could not confuse this town with the university towns of legend, growing forever mossier, receiving and sending out again bright and chosen youth while it remained unchanged and serene: this was something different.) It would have no direction save round about itself, and it would whirl, slowly or swiftly, and in the center of the vortex would be the hollow, the spot of death which he had sensed. And McAllister had this spot, too, the constant inch between his rib and his heart, which he cherished.

But as for himself, he would come to death, but he would *come* to it; he would reach it at the end of a direction and it would not be borne about within him.

Tu quoque: the town and McAllister were older than he.

And so he had them well in their place, safely where they could do him no harm. The town certainly was now but a thing to contemplate, a thing for which he could even anticipate, when he had left it, sharp and pleasant nostalgias, but it was no longer a thing that could hurt or shake him. Somehow, McAllister was a little harder to set aside. Once there had been a McAllister alive in him. When had that been? Three years ago? Much less. He remembered that his friends had known about that McAllister in him and had used to smile in friendly derision. But now the absurd McAllister was dead within him and the real McAllister could not touch him.

Yes, he was free of McAllister and of the town. Their values and thoughts were not his, and there was no compulsion that they be his. He was free of the terrible senility into which they had pushed him. And he was free from the need for their kind of youth. . . .

Beneath his window he saw McAllister in talk with another student. The boy talked to his companion with easy camaraderie but his eyes glanced off over the lake. And suddenly the teacher, as he looked down at his student, felt return all the weariness, all the flatness, all the misery of old age which so elaborately he had fought off. McAllister was dead and done with. But there he stood in his green, irrelevant, unreal youth. And the teacher, looking down at the student, passionately denied all the logic he had used to strangle what had been left of the green, irrelevant, unreal youth in himself. For a little while, for another year, it might still linger with him. Might it not? Ah, indeed, why might it not?

He did not yet want the heavy weight, never to be shaken off, of the real; he did not want the burden of the good and peaceful things, of the necessary terrible things. He wanted yet to spin out a world. He did not want the burden and weight of good peace; he wanted to woo, in the way of youth (at once sick and healthy), defeat and bitterness and high suffering, without the knowledge, fast creeping in upon him, of what they truly were.

A slow fountain of sickly despair rose up in his breast; but it fell as a wave of completest exasperation which overcame him, gripping his vitals, constricting his lungs. How had he ever allowed himself to fall into this thinking? And swiftly he tried to arrange his mind properly: he was over-dramatizing the natural vague sadness which near departure from any place brings; he had, merely, fixed a natural and diffuse emotion upon a wrong and stupid object.

II

As he rose, he knocked his ankle against one of the boxes of books, and with his toe sent it in hearty retaliation sliding along the floor to the wall. From below his window, halting suddenly his anger, a timid questioning greeting quavered cheerfully.

"Hello-o-o-o?"

He had forgotten, supposing that she had not meant it, for she was really quite shy, when she had said she would call up to him that morning as she rode by.

Again, "Hello-o-o-o *there?*" she called in her clear toneless voice which, though he sometimes tried, he never could remember. The window was open, but he struggled with the wire screen so that he could lean out.

"Hello, wait a minute."

He disengaged the screen and rested his arms on the broad stone ledge. She was strange in her white breeches and black boots, her shirt open at her long neck. He had never seen her riding before. She did not sit the horse well, and he knew that, with indifferent acceptance, she was always being thrown. The masculine costume, unbecoming to her, and the unease with which she sat her horse, made her, because of the indubitable and traditional beauty of her slim face, an amusing and appealing drollery. It was as though a newspaper cartoonist had reproduced pervertedly a famous classic picture to illustrate some modern topical point: Gioconda with a mustache, labeled "The Republican National Chairman," smiles and is captioned, "What is he thinking of?"

"How are you?" he said.

"I'm all right. How are *you?*"

"I'm all right."

They were not, by this, sparring for something to say. By the mockery they put into their tone, she a little stiffly as though repeating a learned technique, they were indicating to each other that they quite knew they had nothing to say and that it did not much worry them. It was a ritual well established by now.

"You never saw me riding before, did you?"

"No. You look sort of funny."

"Don't I, though?"

"Nicely funny, of course."

"Just funny."

"Don't contradict me. Those clothes make you look all *gauche* like a willow dryad made accessible." He did not even shudder. It was the only possible way he found to talk to her and he wanted to talk to her.

As always, she was set a little at a loss by this kind of speech, but she liked it and smiled, as now, with a far-off defensive irony. Archly she said, "I don't think I've been very inaccessible."

"I'm not talking about what you are. I'm talking about what you look like. You're like Beauty (capital B) in a house apron."

The word beauty annoyed her. The one thing she was sure of, the one thing that she was remarkable for, the one thing she was indifferent to, was her beauty.

"And don't tell me that you often wear a house apron," he continued, "I know you're domestic and it's something I could never understand. It's ridiculous."

"Why must you quarrel now? I think it's mean of you." She was not continuing the banter, but was quite serious. If he scolded her for not eating enough, if he was annoyed when she insisted on walking in the wet and would not let him call a taxi, she would become hurt and silent.

"I'm going home tomorrow, Enid." He used a lightened, emptied voice, the sort of voice for gay sentimentality in a comedy.

"Yes; I know." Her gentle, passionless regret was so immediate and true that he was ashamed, for he had made the remark only to see how she would look.

"Isn't it ghastly luck?—rain all Spring nearly, and now just the week before I go all this gloriousness to make me want to stay."

He had put off departure for a week and had loitered about the campus fast being deserted, vacantly resting, letting his mind loll, letting his nerves slip loose. The town and the university, which all year at intervals had tried him and fretted him, had become in the week broad and easeful. He had not striven, had not questioned or been curious, but had walked in the fields, along shaded streets, alone or with this lovely girl who had never said a thing illuminating or allowed him to.

"Are you only sorry to leave the weather?"

"You know better than that. You were the best part of the gloriousness."

She said, "Thank you," demurely.

There was a not uncomfortable silence and then she said suddenly, "Listen, I'm not paying for this horse to have him stand under your window. I'm going."

"Good-bye. I'll call for you tonight at seven. Have a nice ride, but don't get your nose sunburned. It'll be last look."

He should not have said that, and as he watched her turn her horse with some difficulty and ride off, unerectly, along the brown lake road, he was sorry that there had been that dull barrier always between them. It was like a barrier of glass, neither could see it but both could feel it. His constant refusal to shatter it had been, he knew, a constant insult to her which he regretted and wanted to apologize for. The reasons for its presence were obvious to him and almost too simple to be canvassed. Two people had said of her that she was the most beautiful girl at the university, and the adjective and the absolute which lay in the superlative had captured him. Never, he recalled, had he known a beautiful girl, a "the most beautiful girl." He had seen her before the phrase had been used of her and had found her faintly attractive; when he heard the phrase and heard it repeated, it had become important that he establish a relationship between him and her.

He had wanted her to be nothing else but what the phrase contained; indeed, perhaps he wanted her to be nothing else but the phrase itself. But the necessity for her being something more became, of course, immediately obvious. She was a person incontestably if not considerably, and she refused to be merely beautiful. After the formality of early acquaintance had worn off, her resistance against being made a symbolic bibelot became pronounced. He feared that there would be dull meetings if he had to regard her as more. But no symbol can long exist merely as the indication of one thing; it begins to take on meanings for itself and begins to have powers beyond the power of the thing it represents. There were dull meetings enough, but he found that he did not mind the dullness. She led him into the most impossible sort of talk and he did not mind, into the most absurd gestures and he regarded them with equanimity. For impossible talk and absurd gestures were the concession he made to prevent anything significant in him from coming beneath the consideration of her sweet and commonplace mind.

But oddly enough, she had been the partial source of moments which, even after long consideration of them, were what he would call "valid" and there was one that he particularly liked to remember. The day, after an infinitude of gray, cold days—Spring mocked and overcome—was fine. In the manner he had and detested, he had wasted the morning in puttering and spleen. In the afternoon he gave a good class; she had come to listen to him and he had spoken with a vivacity that delighted him. Later he met and took her to tea, and then they had gone out on the lake drifting in a canoe. The conversation had been dull, of course, but not irksome. They had stayed so late that each missed the dinner hour, and they dined together in the town. She, perhaps only to discover if he could see her so long in one day (for she knew that he made a formal observance of seeing her which she did not understand), had suggested that they meet after the seminar at which he was due that evening, and he, because so much of the day had been given over to idleness that the whole of it might as well be, had agreed. At the seminar he had spoken well, it was thought, and he had stood up to the professor on an interpretive point, knowing with a keen certainty that he was right. After, they had met and had sat on a ruined landing stage by the lake. When he left, he climbed the hill and sat on the stone exedra. He sat facing the lighted Capitol, looking down at it through the long avenue of young-leafed elms rustling slightly, and at the tight, comfortable city. A train whistled and he could even hear the impatient clash of its cars when it stopped as, fussily, like a dowager getting into a tight skirt, it adjusted itself. Her scent still clung in his nostrils. Her crisp, indubitably beautiful face, too crisp and sharply outlined to be likened to a flower and which was therefore like a wrought cup, as it caught the moonlight and laughed, was clear to him. He was gently glad for all the kisses, his arms were grateful for her slenderness, and he could feel burning intermittently the spot on his neck that she had kissed. A good class, a good argument, caresses returned: and he felt a sort of strength, a definiteness of place in the world. Yet she was not what he wanted, it was all an odd little religious pantomime that he had devised, and a diversion and dissipation of feeling and strength. And he felt the old sense of sin, simple: a duty undone, the morning wasted, and for all the success of his argument he knew that he did not know enough Kant.

Then, suddenly, and for a short moment, the comfort and the strength, the worry and sin, the Capitol, the elms, the city and the university and the clashing noise of the train blended into one single sense of fitness, aptness, and justness:—struggle and strength, bothersomeness but a mind to know and understand, the tragedy of annoyance but strength and love for and a pride in himself; and supporting it all a place that was his, that had meaning for him, a nation, strangely, in whose center he was and he could feel it spreading on all sides of him, and, strangely again, America. Shortly the feeling became confused and never, afterwards, was he able to bring it into the current of his life, but for the moment it lasted it was clear, true and important. He cherished the moment though he could not use it, and for it he found a gratitude to the girl, though her part in it was but small and not glorious.

He would, he knew, when he said good-bye to her, feel a more than conventional regret. She touched him at but one point, and the contact, so far as he could see, was but little important, but he would be hurt by more than the mere breaking of a habit. Perhaps it was only the regret for an unfinished, though unfinishable thing. If so, that was good. It could then go in with the rest of the things that he could not now finish—stupid remarks that should have been set right, hard books that probably he would never return to, half-made friendships, the incomplete image of himself that he was leaving behind—and he would stare at them long enough until they would all become indistinct and properly trivial. . . .

A heap of letters lay on the bed, done into bunches with string. He smiled ruefully as he brought them to the fireplace. One came away thinking that a year's absence would surely do to slough off the outworn friends who kept one talking in the dead jargon of one's past; out of habit or weak, regretful kindness one writes a single letter; it is answered and somehow the volleying begins. Each pile of letters was a friendly little rope to make him on his return tread all the stale old steps. Not even the melodrama of departure in Spring and of return to an old place could quite obscure for him the clear knowledge of what he was returning to. For a sharp moment he felt the long routine of worry to which he was returning, which, if it continued for as long as well it might, could be the instrument of gradual, deject tragedy. There was the worry of these friends of the letters, ripe for discard whom he would not be able to cast off but he would continue to dance to their tunes; there was the worry of the necessary friends who had sunk deep hooks into him that could painfully tear forth for regard his worth and unworth; there was the worry of competition; there was the worry of the justification of self and of the assertion of self; there was the worry of the very noise of New York. But beyond all these components and not to be equaled by any number of conceivable components was the whole: worry—a constant incipient retching; the image of blank, deep, black rest always before the mind and the mind leaning always toward it from the tight bleak fatigue; the sagging at the arms and shoulders as the whole body sought to constrict itself to the navel, sought to be integral and invisible in a point. . . .

Tonight Enid would ask him was he certainly not coming back, as she had asked him many times before. He would enumerate the possibilities for his return and against it and with her weigh them against each other. There were, indeed, no possibilities of return, but it would make the parting less sharp, and he would find it pleasant, as he had before, to feel that there was still the chance to stay at this place which now he could only see as broad and easeful and which, when a fuller control of it were gained, could always be so. But he would not come back.

III

Jew?

The question, mute as Harpo Marx, poked in an idiot face crowned with red curls. (What had happened to the red-haired Jews? Once all Jews had red hair, Judas-like.) It was a routine comedy question now: it slid across the stage with crazy-mad savagery on its idiot face, made play of choking him tremendously. But he did not respond with the conventional gurglings and the exaggerated convulsions that were his part. He was passive and considerably bored.

Mythical characters are careerists, he knew. Ulysses in the first myths was but a picaro, sniveling and sly, red-haired (like Judas, Juan and Satan). Later he had become ennobled into his Homeric state. Later still he had become just too terribly ennobled, by Tennyson, famous ennobler. So with the question: Jew? A new transmuting Tennyson, he had beautifully ennobled that question. He had made an angel of that question, a pet angel, and kept it by for a wrestling workout every now and then, so that he could appear in company pale and worn, with a strange transcendent light, and when people asked the cause of this heroic-seeming weariness he could say, "I have just come from wrestling with my angel of Jewish solitude. It is nothing, this pallor. A little faint I may be, but how strong is my soul. It is good of you to inquire and I like you for it, but should you try to approach and to touch me you would find that you would be kept back by a ring of repelling force emanating from where his arms have circled me. Ah yes, such it is to have an angel in the closet."

It was with scarcely any dismay that he watched the angel become a red-haired comedian. This, he knew, was the fate of all active angels. If mythical characters are careerists they must, after the eminence is reached, suffer the danger of fall. Thus we have Lucifer into Satan rowling in the gulph, Satan rowling in the gulph into a capering imp pitchforking souls into the pasteboard Hellmouth of a morality, an imp capering at Hellmouth into a pantaloon with a red-hot poker. He did not disdain his comedian, liked him rather, and though he was bored by him a little would not quite part with him. Would not part with him? Could not, of course? Perhaps it were better that he have the clown about him than the angel. For it was amazing how often the question asked itself: Jew? Mechanically, for the resolution of many other questions, it presented itself. As a habit it had become dull, but as a habit it had become necessary. And as the shy, half-blind soul of Emerson came to love Rabelais and to scorn Bronson Alcott (an angel with goose-feather wings), so he began to know that it was better to have around him the clown and not the angel. It was better; it gave him more time for himself; he was not a one for angels.

Jew? Yes. All right. Jew. He was bored but obedient as he answered the question.

Was that why McAllister was dead, and why so formally he had made unsuccessful trial of Enid's certain beauty, saying to it the things one said to classic, certain beauty, and why he was leaving here to return to an endless, nagging, worry? Perhaps. Yes.

And he did not know the reason for this. There was, indeed, no reason. If his grandfather should see him in a fancy dress costume, the old man would not disapprove; merely he would shrug his shoulders to suggest, "What for?" Jews did not do such things. Exactly what Jews did he did not know. . . .

The murderous comedian sat down beside him. Lightly he plunged his fingers into the false red curls and regarded the mad head, now quiet and without intent. He looked into the face as deeply as he could; the face gave no look in return; there was no meaning in it for him. Scanning longer and further, the possibility of meaning became less. The eyes were dead; the mouth was idiot as it dreamed upon itself. The hands that had choked for him the pretty dreams of pretty bravery, that had choked for him the assured Renaissance beauty and the pretty things one said to it, dangled between the comic knees. The hands had turned him from this place which, eventually but almost certainly, would have given him a very sweet and gracious contentment. They now dangled between the comic knees, quiet and without purpose. They had done their work and now it seemed doubtful if ever again they would have work to do upon him. They had stripped him of an encumbering finery; without it he felt rough and churlish, but knew that his arms were free.

Free. But free for what? The hands had stripped him for freedom, but they had put no weapon into his own hands, nor yet
pointed out any adversary. He turned to the face beneath the red
hair that he still clutched lightly, to see if, by a longer regard,
some significance might yet be found, some weapon somewhere
hidden might be hinted, some adversary promised him. He looked
deep into the face, contracting all his wits into the keenness of the
look, loosening with a great effort all his sensitivity to receive what
the look would find. Staring, his mind became a single perceptive
blade, his body one apprehensive nerve. There must be some word,
even unformed, upon those lips; there must be some glance in
those old eyes, to tell him where to go, what to resist, what to make:
his faith in that necessity was complete. Tighter and tighter he
clutched the crepe hair in his effort to comprehend unformed word
or veiled and dubious glance. Neither word nor glance came to
him. The face remained blank and idiot. He relaxed his clutch but
let his hand rest upon the red head. . . .

The hands between the comic knees had stripped him but had
given him nothing. The idiot face had leered with a destroying
understanding, but had indicated nothing. It was, after all, as well.
True, he had expected a weapon. But comedians are not armorers.
From the angel he had got solitude. From the comedian he had
got naked freedom, had got a clean-wiped slate, had got the readiness and ability to receive reality.

But it was not enough: freedom must act, a *tabula rasa* exists for
marks to give meaning to its virgin blankness; the readiness to receive and the ability to receive wither, if soon they do not receive. He
could not wait very long in this state of readiness which the comedian had made.

Soon, and very soon, he would have to find his own weapon, his
own adversary, his own thing to do, and this red-haired figure that
crouched by his side would have no part in his finding. Good

enough! The comedian would not part from him; it would wake from its lethargy to make a murderous pass now and then; but these awakenings and these passes would be only funny and numbered among many other funny things. Gérard de Nerval led about a lobster on a blue ribbon; he said that it did not bark and knew the secrets of the deep.

He was not elated, not happy. Indeed, a finger of fear pressed lightly on his brain. He was ready and anxious but not very eager, not avid. He felt old, wise about nothing, flat—deflated and wrinkled like a toy balloon. Some day he would be filled and would become full if the chances were with him. But the prospect did not excite him.

Yet, above elation, above happiness, above eagerness and heroism, and above their absence, rode high and unnoisily a new feeling, scarcely felt, not yet usable. Vaguely he knew what it was; boldly, for a name was needed to call it forth and make it plain, he gave it names. These fixed it but did not explain it. That comment upon it that pleased him best was, "Well, it's about time it came. It's about time."

He felt not happy, not eager, not sternly strong, but complete. He was complete not as a story is complete that a writer sends to the printer, but as the idea for that story becomes complete in the mind of the writer over many months; for the idea will come to the writer perhaps as a bald sentence, a mere static situation, and as it rests in his mind it begins to take on little additions of significance, dropping some and cultivating others, growing and forming itself until the writer finds it sufficiently full to begin to translate on paper. And as the writer sits down to the paper he knows and is afraid that, however complete and promising seemed the idea, words will perhaps betray it, will probably expose it cruelly, will certainly change it, and so he writes with the probability of failure on his pencil. But as he sits down, though he is not elated nor happy, nor has he time for any posture of heroism in the face of this fear, he knows that his thus sitting down and beginning his first paragraph is the only thing he can do and the best moment of his life.

The Lesson and the Secret

(From *Harper's Bazaar*, 1945)

THE nine women of the Techniques of Creative Writing Group sat awaiting the arrival of their instructor, Vincent Hammell. He was not late but they were early and some of them were impatient. The room they sat in was beautiful and bright; its broad windows looked out on the little lake around which the buildings of the city's new cultural center were grouped. The women were disposed about a table of plate glass and their nine handbags lay in an archipelago upon its great lucid surface.

Mrs. Stocker said, "Mr. Hammell isn't here, it seems." There was the intention of irony in her voice—she put a querulous emphasis on the "seems."

Miss Anderson said, "Oh, but it's that we are early—because of our being at the luncheon." She glanced for confirmation at the watch on her wrist.

"Perhaps so," Mrs. Stocker said. "But you know, Constance—speaking metaphorically, Hammell is *not here,* he—is—just—not—here."

At this remark there were nods of considered agreement. Mrs. Territt said, "I think so too. I agree," and brought the palm of her hand down upon her thigh in a sharp slap of decision.

Mrs. Stocker ignored this undesirable ally. She went on, "Not really *here* at all. Oh, I grant you that he is brilliant in a theoretical sense. But those of us who come here"—she spoke tenderly, as if referring to a sacrifice in a public cause—"those of us who come here, come for practice, not for theory. You can test the matter very easily—you can test it by results. And you know as well as I do, Constance, that—there—are—just—no—results—at—all."

Miss Anderson had gone through uprisings like this every spring and she knew that there was no standing against Mrs. Stocker. Mrs. Stocker would have her own way, especially since the group that opposed her was so small and uncourageous, consisting, in addition to Miss Anderson herself, only of Mrs. Knight and Miss Wilson. Young Mrs. Knight was extremely faithful and quite successful in carrying out the class assignments and this naturally put her under suspicion of being prejudiced in favor of the instructor. Her opinion was bound to be discounted. As for Miss Wilson, her presence in the group was generally supposed to have merely the therapeutic purpose of occupying her unhappy mind. It was not a frequent presence, for she shrank from society, and now she looked miserably away from the insupportable spectacle of anyone's being blamed for anything whatsoever.

Miss Anderson said, "But surely we can't blame that all on Mr. Hammell."

"No, not all," Mrs. Stocker conceded handsomely because it was so little to concede. "I grant you it isn't *all* his fault. But I think we have the right to expect—. It isn't as if we weren't paying. And generously, too, I might add. And there's nothing to show. Not one of us has sold herself."

Mrs. Territt gave vent to an explosive snicker. At once Mrs. Stocker traced the reason for the outburst to Mrs. Territt's primitive sexual imagination and said sharply, "Not one of us has sold herself to a single magazine. Not one of us has put herself across."

Of the nine women, all were very wealthy. They made Vincent Hammell's first experience of wealth, and nothing he had learned from books had prepared him for what he found. It seemed to Vincent that only in the case of Miss Anderson had wealth been a true condition of life, shaping and marking her as nothing else could have done. She alone bore something of the imagined appearance of wealth, the serenity and disinterestedness to which wealth is supposed ideally to aspire.

Vincent supposed that either the size or the age or the nature of Miss Anderson's fortune had led her—as fortunes of a kind sometimes do—into a historical lapse, an aberration of her sense of time. For Miss Anderson, although not "old-fashioned" nor long past her youth, seemed not to inhabit quite the same present in which her friends lived. She seemed, indeed, to live in reference to certain delicate points of honor such as Edith Wharton, but few after her, would have been concerned with. Vincent assumed, for example, that some high moral decision, its meaning now obscured, accounted for the unmarried state of a woman so pleasant as Miss Anderson. It was surely to be laid to some sacrifice of herself, some service of an idea. The idea which she served would not have to be very complex or important, but still it was an idea. Perhaps this explained the historical impression she made, for to many people the present consists of things, while the past consists of ideas. Like the past, Miss Anderson was a failure. Yet in some way she continued to exist with a gentle unsought authority which perhaps came from her friends' dim response to the power of the idea and their recognition of the magical, if limited, potency of the past; she was not aggressive or competitive and it was felt that she shed a justification upon whatever groups she joined.

Now and then Miss Anderson submitted to Vincent's criticisms the stories she wrote. They were elaborate and literate—well written, the class called them—but they had no relation to any reality Vincent could identify. In the world of Miss Anderson's stories, servants were old and loyal; wives hid nameless diseases from their husbands or silently bore the most torturing infidelities, or found themselves hideously in the power of depraved lovers; memories played a great part, the memories of single passionate nights or of single significant phrases, and it sometimes happened that flowers or white gloves were forever cherished. When Vincent discussed these stories with Miss Anderson, he was always surprised at the small conviction with which he spoke about their lack of reality—he almost believed, as he spoke to her, that there might actually be such a world beyond his strict modern knowledge.

The distinction which Miss Anderson had was perhaps but a weak one, yet it gave Vincent Hammell a standard by which he could fairly measure the inadequacy of her colleagues. If she did not carry the power of her position, she at least carried its tragic consciousness. Wealth and position, Vincent felt, should appear in their proper forms and add to the variety of life. He was sure that there were proper forms both of refinement and vulgarity. But these women made but a commonplace spectacle. Thus, the meager taste in dress of Mrs. Stocker quite matched the meagerness of her face, which showed the irritable energy of a person whose social self-esteem is not matched by cash in the bank. Or Mrs. Territt was so very coarse in complexion, so drab in dress and so brutally dull in manner that it was inevitable to suppose that what gentility she had was hanging only by a thread of income. Mrs. Knight was ruddy and healthy from an expensive outdoor life, but in other respects she appeared no more than merely well off. Poor Miss Wilson's truly painful nervousness and her evasive eye quite transcended the bounds of class.

Yet on the other hand, it was even more difficult to believe in the actual status of Mrs. Broughton, Mrs. Forrester and old Mrs. Pomeroy, for wealth had marked them only in the way of parody and they were all so "typical" that one had to suppose that they had been produced not so much by nature and circumstance as by certain artistic imaginations of rather limited range. Vincent felt that in the East, in New York or Boston, cities of complex culture, wealth would surely make a better show, would impart a more firmly bottomed assurance, a truer arrogance. Then, too, he could suppose that these women were the failures and misfits of their class, else they would not have to meet weekly to devote themselves to literature.

"I have nothing against Hammell personally, nothing whatsoever," Mrs. Stocker said. "What I think is that we need a different *kind* of person. Hammell is very modern, but we need somebody more practical. It seems to me that if we could have a literary agent, who could give us the straight dope, tell us about contacts and the right approach . . ."

Mrs. Stocker had no need to complete her conditional clause. The straight dope, the contacts and the right approach, went directly to the hearts of Mrs. Territt, Mrs. Broughton, and Mrs. Forrester. They murmured a surprised approval of the firm originality of the suggestion. Even old Mrs. Pomeroy raised her eyebrows to indicate that although human nature did not change, it sometimes appeared in interesting new aspects. To all the ladies, indeed, it came as a relief that Mrs. Stocker should suggest that there was another secret than that of creation. There was a power possibly more efficacious, the secret of selling, of contacts and the right approach.

Miss Anderson said, "But aren't all the literary agents in New York?" She said it tentatively, for she was without worldly knowledge, but what she said was so sensibly true that the general enthusiasm was dampened.

"But surely," Mrs. Stocker said, and her voice was almost desperate, "but surely there must be somebody?"

Mrs. Broughton, who was staring out of the window, said, "Here he comes," whispering it like a guilty conspiratorial schoolgirl. Mrs. Forrester closed her dark expressive eyes to the group to signal "mum" and the ladies composed their faces.

Could Vincent Hammell have heard the conversation of which

he was the subject, he would have been surprised by only one element in it—the lack of any response to him personally. He knew he was not succeeding with the group, but he knew, too, that none of the instructors who had come before him had succeeded any better. The university had sent its best men, professors first, then young assistants likely to be more modern. Each autumn the new man had been received with taut feminine expectancy; each spring he had been discarded, for he had not conveyed the precious, the inconceivable secret which the women had come in hopes to receive. Yet though Hammell might understand that he was not successful, he always supposed that he was a little forgiven by reason of his sex and age. He was wrong to count on this feminine extenuation—his masculinity and youth made his case, if anything, even worse.

His failure had no doubt begun when, upon being invited to instruct the group, he had conjured up a vision of gently bred ladies, all pretty and all precisely thirty years old, gracefully filling empty days and hearts with the delicate practice of a craft humbly loved. He had not been prepared for the urgent women who were actually his pupils, nor for their grim dark worship of the potency that print conferred, nor for their belief—more intense than any coterie in metropolitan garrets could have—that they were held in bondage by a great conspiracy of editors.

Vincent Hammell was carrying his brief-case, an elegant piece of luggage of excellent leather and the best bronze hardware. It had been a gift from his parents, who, with such gifts, useful but very fine and extravagant, kept for themselves and their son the memory and hope of better days. Vincent was glad of the brief-case, for it helped to arm his youth and poverty against the wealth and years of his pupils. He laid it on the plate-glass table beneath which his own legs and the legs of the women were visible. He opened it and took out a thin folder of manuscript. Miss Anderson cleared her throat, caught the eye of member after member and brought the meeting to order. Hammell looked up and took over the class. It was only his entrance into the room that gave him trouble and now he spoke briskly and with authority.

"Two weeks ago," he said, "I asked you to write an account of some simple outdoor experience. You were to concentrate on the physical details. You remember we discussed as models a passage from *Huckleberry Finn* and a story of Ernest Hemingway's." He picked up the folder of manuscript and examined its thinness. "Some of you," he said drily, "carried out the assignment."

Mrs. Stocker moved in her seat to signalize a protest which Vincent understood—all this was elementary. "I'd like to read one example," he said.

He took a manuscript from the folder. Only three of the women had attempted the assignment, two of them dully. But he was rather proud of Mrs. Knight's little story. It was quite unpretentious, about a young wife who is left by her husband in their hunting lodge in the Canadian woods. She wakes in the night to hear a howling that can be only that of wild animals and then the creaking hinge of an unlatched door opening and closing. She is not alone, but of the two guests one is another woman and the man is incompetent. She lies still and miserable, bearing all the sad isolation of responsibility; the conflict of her emotions is not between fear of the beasts and the impulse to protect herself, but rather between fear of the beasts and fear of her husband's contempt for her lack of courage. But at last she becomes bold—and finds that though indeed the door is unlatched, the howling is only that of a high wind. It was perhaps not entirely convincing that she should have deceived herself, but something in the manner of the story was indeed convincing, her desire to seem manly to her husband and the whole impulse of the story itself to discover safety where danger had been imagined.

Vincent began to read this story aloud. Just then the door opened and two women came in. They made little gestures of greeting to their friends and politely indicated, by exhibiting how they were out of breath, that their lateness had been unavoidable. Vincent waited for them to settle and then again began to read. When he came to the end, he paused for a while and looked around the table.

"What do you think of it?" he asked.

"Very nice," Mrs. Broughton said. "Very nice indeed." Mrs. Broughton, it always seemed to Vincent, had been imagined by a radical caricaturist of rather conventional fancy. Careless of verisimilitude, concerned only with the political passions he would arouse, the artist had drawn her short and pudgy, with a face of gross and foolish pride and a bridling neck which gave an air of condenscension to her remarks, many of which were in their intention really quite good-natured. Mrs. Knight was not gratified by Mrs. Broughton's praise.

"Yes, it is very nice," Mrs. Stocker said, suppressing as much as she could the condescension she felt. "Of course, it has no plot, no complication, no conflict really, but it has a kind of twist at the end, it is true to life and it has touches of realism."

"Oh, very realistic," said Mrs. Broughton.

"Well, I don't think it *is* very realistic," said Mrs. Forrester with sudden authority. As compared with the inventor of Mrs. Broughton, the imagination that had conceived Mrs. Forrester was of greater complexity—some social satirist, gifted but not profound, had projected this elegant woman, not young but still beautiful, and had endowed her with an intensity of self-regard and a sense of noblesse so petulant and shoulder-shrugging, yet so easily snubbed, that poor Mrs. Forrester lived in a constant alternation of blind attack and bewildered retreat, with the result that since her beautiful girlhood scarcely anyone had felt toward her any emotion save the various degrees of contempt. "Not at all—to me it doesn't seem at all realistic." She held her pretty head high to front the refutation which her judgments inevitably and bewilderingly provoked. "It isn't *convincing,*" she said. "Now take the central problem—yes, take the central *problem*. That definitely is *not* convincing. She lies there worrying about what she should do. *Why? What for?"*—her appeal was vehement. "All she had to do was ring for the guides, and that would be *that!*" Her beautiful dark eyes flashed finality.

There was a gasp from Mrs. Knight. Her cheeks flamed. She almost rose from her chair. Her voice was choked. "It just so happens," she said with terrible scorn, "it just so happens that she couldn't ring for the guides because in our lodge—there—are—no—guides—to—ring for."

The group was wholly with Mrs. Knight in the matter. As usual, Mrs. Forrester was silenced.

Mrs. Stocker said, "Mr. Hammell, I gather that you like that story of Mrs. Knight's. And I like it too. It has a very fresh quality, definitely fresh. But the question I want to ask is whether in your opinion a story like that has a marketable value."

There were little nods around the table as the spirit of the junta asserted itself once more, but there was a constraining sense of guilt now that Vincent Hammell was here. Mrs. Knight looked very conscious. She was humble about her writing and near enough to her college days to submit to the discipline of an assigned exercise, but she was naturally not averse to knowing whether or not she had produced a commodity.

"Now you take Constance's stories—Miss Anderson's stories, Mr. Hammell. You yourself admit that they have something. They're well thought out and they're well written, they have suspense and a twist at the end. But the editors just never take them."

Miss Anderson looked up in surprise and unhappiness. Although now and then she sent her stories to market, she seemed to feel no chagrin at their refusal.

"Now why do you think that is, Mr. Hammell?" Mrs. Stocker said. There was a silence, a degree of attention that Hammell saw the significance in. He considered how to answer. Miss Anderson looked withdrawn from the inquisition.

Mrs. Broughton broke the silence. "It's because they are refined and charming and what they want nowadays is coarse—and middle class. About miners. There was a story I read about two children who could hear each other practicing the piano through the walls of their apartment." She tossed her head in resentment. "Who cares?"

Mrs. Territt broke in and her coarse voice was injured and defensive. She said, "You all talk about selling stories. What I want to know is how to write them. That's what I came here to find out." She looked hostilely at Vincent. "All this talk about what's been done already! I came here to learn *how to do it at all!*"

Three or four women were swayed by this utterance to confess among themselves what they had never before realized. "Yes, yes," they murmured and nodded to each other. The group was now divided between those who believed that the secret lay in learning to sell and those who believed that it lay in learning to write.

"Personally," Mrs. Territt said, and her glance at Hammell was now malevolent, "personally, that is what I give up my time to come here for. And I haven't got it—*nothing.*" The murmur of agreement she had won had gone to her head and she was breathing hard.

Vincent said, "Mrs. Territt, one can only learn to write by writing." For the fact was that Mrs. Territt had never yet submitted a manuscript.

She bridled. "I suppose that's very smart." She used the word *smart* not in the English sense of something clean and precise or fashionable and elegant but in the old American sense of something clever and impertinent. In the eyes of all present this declassed her.

Vincent said, "How long do you spend at your desk every day, Mrs. Territt?"

She did not answer but looked sullenly at the table before her.

"Four hours a day?" Vincent said inexorably. He could feel the solidifying interest of the group. The many handsomely shod feet seen through the top of the table looked like aquarial creatures as they shifted a little with interest.

"Three hours? Two? One solid hour every day?"

Mrs. Territt was sulking like a scolded chambermaid with an inexpressible grievance. Suddenly she flashed out, "No, why should I? When I never get any ideas?" It was a direct accusation against Hammell.

Someone snickered and no doubt the fight was won, but Hammell went on: "How long do you spend every day trying to get ideas?"

She looked at him blankly from her raging sulks.

It was necessary to bring the matter to an end. Vincent took a book from his brief-case. It was a volume of stories by a writer he much admired, Garda Thorne. "Shall we continue the class?" he said. The women nodded.

Vincent began to read aloud the story he had selected. It was about two young American girls who were visiting friends in an Austrian village. They were Catholics and they were sent by their hostess to pay a call of ceremony on the priest of the village. The priest had received them charmingly, he was very polite. He was in an especially good humor because the new wine from the grapes of his own little arbor was just ready. It stood in his tin bathtub on the floor. Just as the visit began, the priest was urgently sent for. He begged his young guests to remain until his return. They could not but agree, yet as his absence continued they sat there bored and impatient and wondering how to amuse themselves until first one and then the other took off her shoes and stockings, held her skirts high and stepped into the tub. If you stopped to think of it, it was not quite probable, but it was a wonderfully funny and charming picture, the first girl standing in the wine, then the second, then both together, elegantly dressed and with their wide straw hats on, the drops of red wine splashing up to their thighs, their white feet and ankles scarcely visible to themselves as they looked down into the roiled wine.

Then there was the scramble to get themselves decent before the priest should come home, the scrubbing with inadequate handkerchiefs, the sanding of the soapstone floor to clean off the prints of their feet. When the priest returned they had to sit there demure, with their legs still sticky under their stockings. The priest served them the wine they had bathed in and their manners were perfect as they heard him say that never had he known the wine to be so good.

As the story went on to its end, Vincent was sorry he had chosen it to read. The silence was becoming unusually intense. He had especially wanted Miss Anderson to hear the story, for he thought it might suggest to her, with its simplicity, gaiety and elegance, that there were better subjects than the unreal complexities she so feelingly conceived. But, as he read, he felt that it had been a cruel mistake to read this story to these women. As it went on through its narration of the flash of skirts and underskirts, of white stained thighs, the grave silence of the girls and then their giggles and the beautiful prints of their naked feet on the stone floor, it seemed to him that his own youth had been thoughtless to have chosen the story. He felt, too, like an intruder into feminine mysteries and the sweat came to his forehead. He dreaded the return of the priest and the end of the story when he would have to take his eyes from the book and look around. At last he finished. He did not look up but moodily sifted through the pages of the book. This had the histrionic effect of letting the story hang for a while in the air.

For a moment the silence continued. Then it was broken by Miss Anderson, crying, "Oh that was lovely, Mr. Hammell," and "lovely," "lovely," "lovely," echoed the women around the glass table, beneath whose surface there was a shifting of legs and a pulling down of skirts over knees.

Vincent Hammell now ventured to look at their faces, which were relaxed and benign. There were little half-smiles on their mouths, directed tangentially at him. It was as if he himself had been the author of the story and as if the story had celebrated the things that were their peculiar possessions, their youth, their beauty, their femininity.

In the sunlit room, in the soft spring air, there was a moment of musing silence as the quest for the precious secret was abandoned. Despite himself, Vincent Hammell experienced a sense of power, in all his months of teaching the class the first he had felt. Yet in the entrancement of the women, in their moment of brooding relaxation, there was something archaic and mythological, something latently dangerous. It was thus that the women of Thrace must have sat around Orpheus before they had had occasion to be enraged with him. He would have liked to remind them, but it was not possible, that he had merely read aloud to them the story which a woman, Garda Thorne, had written.

It was old Mrs. Pomeroy who memorialized the moment. Mrs. Pomeroy was by far a gayer creation than either Mrs. Broughton or Mrs. Forrester. Perhaps she was aware of her role, perhaps she had even had the charming wit to invent it herself—she was the old lady of widest experience and profoundest wisdom and it was impossible not to see her lengthy past of drawing rooms (at home and abroad) in which the brilliant and the famous were received. Silence and a twinkle were the evidences of Mrs. Pomeroy's breadth of culture. At certain literary names she would smile, as at the memory of old, intimate and special delights. But only once had she made vocal her feeling for the great past. On that occasion the name of Proust had been mentioned by Vincent Hammell and what Mrs. Pomeroy had said was, "And also Paul Bourget."

She had added a knowledgeable whisper of explanation, "Psychology!" And now, as her way was, she smiled sadly and wisely as she spoke. She closed her eyes and said, "Such a story makes one truly glad there is literature. We should be grateful."

She spoke so seldom and perhaps she was really wise—at her benediction upon literature and her admonition to gratitude everyone looked solemn, as if, in the moving picture, they were listening to Anatole France delivering the panegyric at Zola's funeral.

"Very excellent," said Mrs. Broughton. "Very."

And now Mrs. Stocker spoke. "What I like about the story," she said, "is that it is neither one thing nor another. I mean it isn't highbrow *or* commercial."

It was not that she wanted to bring the discussion back again to the matter which so much interested her. No doubt she as much as anyone else had been caught in the moment of contemplation, but in uttering her feeling about it she used the only language she knew. And having used that language, it was now natural for her to say, "Tell me, Mr. Hammell, does this writer sell well?"

At the question there was a noisy little murmur of agreement to its relevance as the eyes turned to Vincent Hammell to demand his answer.

Of This Time, of That Place

(From *Partisan Review,* 1943)

I T was a fine September day. By noon it would be summer again but now it was true autumn with a touch of chill in the air. As Joseph Howe stood on the porch of the house in which he lodged, ready to leave for his first class of the year, he thought with pleasure of the long indoor days that were coming. It was a moment when he could feel glad of his profession.

On the lawn the peach tree was still in fruit and young Hilda Aiken was taking a picture of it. She held the camera tight against her chest. She wanted the sun behind her but she did not want her own long morning shadow in the foreground. She raised the camera but that did not help, and she lowered it but that made things worse. She twisted her body to the left, then to the right. In the end she had to step out of the direct line of the sun. At last she snapped the shutter and wound the film with intense care.

Howe, watching her from the porch, waited for her to finish and called good morning. She turned, startled, and almost sullenly lowered her glance. In the year Howe had lived at the Aikens', Hilda had accepted him as one of her family, but since his absence of the summer she had grown shy. Then suddenly she lifted her head and smiled at him, and the humorous smile confirmed his pleasure in the day. She picked up her bookbag and set off for school.

The handsome houses on the streets to the college were not yet fully awake but they looked very friendly. Howe went by the Bradby house where he would be a guest this evening at the first dinner-party of the year. When he had gone the length of the picket fence, the whitest in town, he turned back. Along the path there was a fine row of asters and he went through the gate and picked one for his buttonhole. The Bradbys would be pleased if they happened to see him invading their lawn and the knowledge of this made him even more comfortable.

He reached the campus as the hour was striking. The students were hurrying to their classes. He himself was in no hurry. He stopped at his dim cubicle of an office and lit a cigarette. The prospect of facing his class had suddenly presented itself to him and his hands were cold, the lawful seizure of power he was about to make seemed momentous. Waiting did not help. He put out his cigarette, picked up a pad of theme paper and went to his classroom.

As he entered, the rattle of voices ceased and the twenty-odd freshmen settled themselves and looked at him appraisingly. Their faces seemed gross, his heart sank at their massed impassivity, but he spoke briskly.

"My name is Howe," he said and turned and wrote it on the blackboard. The carelessness of the scrawl confirmed his authority. He went on, "My office is 412 Slemp Hall and my office hours are Monday, Wednesday, and Friday from eleven-thirty to twelve-thirty."

He wrote, "M., W., F., 11:30-12:30." He said, "I'll be very glad to see any of you at that time. Or if you can't come then, you can arrange with me for some other time."

He turned again to the blackboard and spoke over his shoulder. "The text for the course is Jarman's *Modern Plays*, revised edition.

The Co-op has it in stock." He wrote the name, underlined "revised edition" and waited for it to be taken down in the new notebooks.

When the bent heads were raised again he began his speech of prospectus. "It is hard to explain—," he said, and paused as they composed themselves. "It is hard to explain what a course like this is intended to do. We are going to try to learn something about modern literature and something about prose composition."

As he spoke, his hands warmed and he was able to look directly at the class. Last year on the first day the faces had seemed just as cloddish, but as the term wore on they became gradually alive and quite likable. It did not seem possible that the same thing could happen again.

"I shall not lecture in this course," he continued. "Our work will be carried on by discussion and we will try to learn by an exchange of opinion. But you will soon recognize that my opinion is worth more than anyone else's here."

He remained grave as he said it, but two boys understood and laughed. The rest took permission from them and laughed too. All Howe's private ironies protested the vulgarity of the joke but the laughter made him feel benign and powerful.

When the little speech was finished, Howe picked up the pad of paper he had brought. He announced that they would write an extemporaneous theme. Its subject was traditional, "Who I am and why I came to Dwight College." By now the class was more at ease and it gave a ritualistic groan of protest. Then there was a stir as fountain-pens were brought out and the writing arms of the chairs were cleared and the paper was passed about. At last all the heads bent to work and the room became still.

Howe sat idly at his desk. The sun shone through the tall clumsy windows. The cool of the morning was already passing. There was a scent of autumn and of varnish, and the stillness of the room was deep and oddly touching. Now and then a student's head was raised and scratched in the old elaborate students' pantomime that calls the teacher to witness honest intellectual effort.

Suddenly a tall boy stood within the frame of the open door. "Is this," he said, and thrust a large nose into a college catalogue, "is this the meeting place of English 1A? The section instructed by Dr. Joseph Howe?"

He stood on the very sill of the door, as if refusing to enter until he was perfectly sure of all his rights. The class looked up from work, found him absurd and gave a low mocking cheer.

The teacher and the new student, with equal pointedness, ignored the disturbance. Howe nodded to the boy, who pushed his head forward and then jerked it back in a wide elaborate arc to clear his brow of a heavy lock of hair. He advanced into the room and halted before Howe, almost at attention. In a loud clear voice he announced, "I am Tertan, Ferdinand R., reporting at the direction of Head of Department Vincent."

The heraldic formality of this statement brought forth another cheer. Howe looked at the class with a sternness he could not really feel, for there was indeed something ridiculous about this boy. Under his displeased regard the rows of heads dropped to work again. Then he touched Tertan's elbow, led him up to the desk and stood so as to shield their conversation from the class.

"We are writing an extemporaneous theme," he said. "The subject is, 'Who I am and why I came to Dwight College.' "

He stripped a few sheets from the pad and offered them to the boy. Tertan hesitated and then took the paper but he held it only tentatively. As if with the effort of making something clear, he gulped, and a slow smile fixed itself on his face. It was at once knowing and shy.

"Professor," he said, "to be perfectly fair to my classmates"—he made a large gesture over the room—"and to you"—he inclined his head to Howe—"this would not be for me an extemporaneous subject."

Howe tried to understand. "You mean you've already thought about it—you've heard we always give the same subject? That doesn't matter."

Again the boy ducked his head and gulped. It was the gesture of one who wishes to make a difficult explanation with perfect candor. "Sir," he said, and made the distinction with great care, "the topic I did not expect but I have given much ratiocination to the subject."

Howe smiled and said, "I don't think that's an unfair advantage. Just go ahead and write."

Tertan narrowed his eyes and glanced sidewise at Howe. His strange mouth smiled. Then in quizzical acceptance, he ducked his head, threw back the heavy dank lock, dropped into a seat with a great loose noise and began to write rapidly.

The room fell silent again and Howe resumed his idleness. When the bell rang, the students who had groaned when the task had been set now groaned again because they had not finished. Howe took up the papers and held the class while he made the first assignment. When he dismissed it, Tetran bore down on him, his slack mouth held ready for speech.

"Some professors," he said, "are pedants. They are Dryasdusts. However, some professors are free souls and creative spirits. Kant, Hegel, and Nietzsche were all professors." With this pronouncement he paused. "It is my opinion," he continued, "that you occupy the second category."

Howe looked at the boy in surprise and said with good-natured irony, "With Kant, Hegel, and Nietzsche?"

Not only Tertan's hand and head but his whole awkward body waved away the stupidity. "It is the kind and not the quantity of the kind," he said sternly.

Rebuked, Howe said as simply and seriously as he could, "It would be nice to think so." He added, "Of course I am not a professor."

This was clearly a disappointment but Tertan met it. "In the French sense," he said with composure. "Generically, a teacher."

Suddenly he bowed. It was such a bow, Howe fancied, as a stage-director might teach an actor playing a medieval student who takes leave of Abelard—stiff, solemn, with elbows close to the body and feet together. Then, quite as suddenly, he turned and left.

A queer fish, and as soon as Howe reached his office he sifted through the batch of themes and drew out Tertan's. The boy had filled many sheets with his unformed headlong scrawl. "Who am I?" he had begun. "Here, in a mundane, not to say commercialized academe, is asked the question which from time long immemorably out of mind has accreted doubts and thoughts in the psyche of man to pester him as a nuisance. Whether in St. Augustine (or Austin as sometimes called) or Miss Bashkirtsieff or Frederic Amiel or Empedocles, or in less lights of the intellect than these, this posed question has been ineluctable."

Howe took out his pencil. He circled "academe" and wrote "vocab," in the margin. He underlined "time long immemorably out of mind" and wrote "Diction!" But this seemed inadequate for what was wrong. He put down his pencil and read ahead to discover the principle of error in the theme. "Today as ever, in spite of gloomy prophets of the dismal science (economics) the question is uninvalidated. Out of the starry depths of heaven hurtles this spear of query demanding to be caught on the shield of the mind ere it pierces the skull and the limbs be unstrung."

Baffled but quite caught, Howe read on. "Materialism, by which is meant the philosophic concept and not the moral idea, provides no aegis against the question which lies beyond the tangible (metaphysics). Existence without alloy is the question presented. Environment and heredity relegated aside, the rags and old clothes of practical life discarded, the name and the instrumentality of livelihood do not, as the prophets of the dismal science insist on in this connection, give solution to the interrogation which not from the professor merely but veritably from the cosmos is given. I think, therefore I am (cogito etc.) but who am I? Tertan I am, but what is Tertan? Of this time, of that place, of some parentage, what does it matter?"

Existence without alloy: the phrase established itself. Howe put aside Tertan's paper and at random picked up another. "I am Arthur J. Casebeer Jr." he read. "My father is Arthur J. Casebeer and my grandfather was Arthur J. Casebeer before him. My mother is Nina Wimble Casebeer. Both of them are college graduates and my father is in insurance. I was born in St. Louis eighteen years ago and we still make our residence there."

Arthur J. Casebeer, who knew who he was, was less interesting than Tertan, but more coherent. Howe picked up Tertan's paper again. It was clear that none of the routine marginal comments, no "sent. str." or "punct." or "vocab." could cope with this torrential rhetoric. He read ahead, contenting himself with underscoring the errors against the time when he should have the necessary "conference" with Tertan.

It was a busy and official day of cards and sheets, arrangements and small decisions, and it gave Howe pleasure. Even when it was time to attend the first of the weekly Convocations he felt the charm of the beginning of things when intention is still innocent and uncorrupted by effort. He sat among the young instructors on the platform and joined in their humorous complaints at having to assist at the ceremony, but actually he got a clear satisfaction from the ritual of prayer and prosy speech and even from wearing his academic gown. And when the Convocation was over the pleasure continued as he crossed the campus, exchanging greetings with men he had not seen since the spring. They were people who did not yet, and perhaps never would, mean much to him, but in a year they had grown amiably to be part of his life. They were his fellow townsmen.

The day had cooled again at sunset and there was a bright chill in the September twilight. Howe carried his voluminous gown over his arm, he swung his doctoral hood by its purple neckpiece and on his head he wore his mortarboard with its heavy gold tassel bobbing just over his eye. These were the weighty and absurd symbols of his new profession and they pleased him. At twenty-six Joseph Howe had discovered that he was neither so well off nor so bohemian as he had once thought. A small income, adequate when supplemented by a sizable cash legacy, was genteel poverty when the cash was all spent. And the literary life—the room at the Lafayette or the small apartment without a lease, the long summers on the Cape, the long afternoons and the social evenings—began to weary him. His writing filled his mornings and should perhaps have filled his life, yet it did not. To the amusement of his friends and with a certain sense that he was betraying his own freedom, he had used the last of his legacy for a year at Harvard. The small but respectable reputation of his two volumes of verse had proved useful—he continued at Harvard on a fellowship and when he emerged as Dr. Howe he received an excellent appointment, with prospects, at Dwight.

He had his moments of fear when all that had ever been said of the dangers of the academic life had occurred to him. But after a year in which he had tested every possibility of corruption and seduction he was ready to rest easy. His third volume of verse, most of it written in his first year of teaching, was not only ampler but, he thought, better than its predecessors.

There was a clear hour before the Bradby dinner-party and Howe looked forward to it. But he was not to enjoy it, for lying with his mail on the hall table was a copy of this quarter's issue of *Life and Letters,* to which his landlord subscribed. Its severe cover announced that its editor, Frederic Woolley, had this month contributed an essay called "Two Poets," and Howe, picking it up, curious to see who the two poets might be, felt his own name start out at him with cabalistic power—Joseph Howe. As he continued to turn the pages his hand trembled.

Standing in the dark hall, holding the neat little magazine, Howe

knew that his literary contempt for Frederic Woolley meant nothing, for he suddenly understood how he respected Woolley in the
way of the world. He knew this by the trembling of his hand. And
of the little world as well as the great, for although the literary
groups of New York might dismiss Woolley, his name carried high
authority in the academic world. At Dwight it was even a revered
name, for it had been here at the college that Frederic Woolley had
made the distinguished scholarly career from which he had gone on
to literary journalism. In middle life he had been induced to take
the editorship of *Life and Letters,* a literary monthly not widely read
but heavily endowed and in its pages he had carried on the defense
of what he sometimes called the older values. He was not without
wit, he had great knowledge and considerable taste and even in the
full movement of the "new" literature he had won a certain respect
for his refusal to accept it. In France, even in England, he would
have been connected with a more robust tradition of conservatism,
but America gave him an audience not much better than genteel. It
was known in the college that to the subsidy of *Life and Letters* the
Bradbys contributed a great part.

As Howe read, he saw that he was involved in nothing less than
an event. When the Fifth Series of *Studies in Order and Value*
came to be collected, this latest of Frederic Woolley's essays would
not be merely another step in the old direction. Clearly and unmis-
takably, it was a turning point. All his literary life Woolley had
been concerned with the relation of literature to morality, religion,
and the private and delicate pieties, and he had been unalterably
opposed to all that he had called "inhuman humanitarianism." But
here, suddenly, dramatically late, he had made an about-face, turning to the public life and to the humanitarian politics he had so long
despised. This was the kind of incident the histories of literature
make much of. Frederic Woolley was opening for himself a new
career and winning a kind of new youth. He contrasted the two
poets, Thomas Wormser who was admirable, Joseph Howe who was

almost dangerous. He spoke of the "precious subjectivism" of Howe's verse. "In times like ours," he wrote, "with millions facing penury and want, one feels that the qualities of the *tour d'ivoire* are well-nigh inhuman, nearly insulting. The *tour d'ivoire* becomes the *tour d'ivresse* and it is not self-intoxicated poets that our people need." The essay said more: "The problem is one of meaning. I am not ignorant that the creed of the esoteric poets declares that a poem does not and should not *mean* anything, that it *is* something. But poetry is what the poet makes it, and if he is a true poet he makes what his society needs. And what is needed now is the tradition in which Mr. Wormser writes, the true tradition of poetry. The Howes do no harm, but they do no good when positive good is demanded of all responsible men. Or do the Howes indeed do no harm? Perhaps Plato would have said they do, that in some ways theirs is the Phrygian music that turns men's minds from the struggle. Certainly it is true that Thomas Wormser writes in the lucid Dorian mode which sends men into battle with evil."

It was easy to understand why Woolley had chosen to praise Thomas Wormser. The long, lilting lines of *Corn Under Willows* hymned, as Woolley put it, the struggle for wheat in the Iowa fields and expressed the real lives of real people. But why out of the dozen more notable examples he had chosen Howe's little volume as the example of "precious subjectivism" was hard to guess. In a way it was funny, this multiplication of himself into "the Howes." And yet this becoming the multiform political symbol by whose creation Frederic Woolley gave the sign of a sudden new life, this use of him as a sacrifice whose blood was necessary for the rites of rejuvenation, made him feel oddly unclean.

Nor could Howe get rid of a certain practical resentment. As a poet he had a special and respectable place in the college life. But it might be another thing to be marked as the poet of a willful and selfish obscurity.

As he walked to the Bradby's Howe was a little tense and defensive. It seemed to him that all the world knew of the "attack" and agreed with it. And indeed the Bradbys had read the essay but Professor Bradby, a kind and pretentious man, said, "I see my old friend knocked you about a bit, my boy," and his wife Eugenia looked at Howe with her childlike blue eyes and said, "I shall *scold* Frederic for the untrue things he wrote about you. You aren't the least obscure." They beamed at him. In their genial snobbery they seemed to feel that he had distinguished himself. He was the leader of Howeism. He enjoyed the dinner-party as much as he had thought he would.

And in the following days, as he was more preoccupied with his duties, the incident was forgotten. His classes had ceased to be mere groups. Student after student detached himself from the mass and required or claimed a place in Howe's awareness. Of them all it was Tertan who first and most violently signaled his separate existence. A week after classes had begun Howe saw his silhouette on the frosted glass of his office door. It was motionless for a long time, perhaps stopped by the problem of whether or not to knock before entering. Howe called, "Come in!" and Tertan entered with his shambling stride.

He stood beside the desk, silent and at attention. When Howe asked him to sit down, he responded with a gesture of head and hand as if to say that such amenities were beside the point. Nevertheless he did take the chair. He put his ragged crammed briefcase between his legs. His face, which Howe now observed fully for the first time, was confusing, for it was made up of florid curves, the nose arched in the bone and voluted in the nostril, the mouth loose and soft and rather moist. Yet the face was so thin and narrow as to seem the very type of asceticism. Lashes of unusual length veiled the eyes and, indeed, it seemed as if there were a veil over the whole countenance. Before the words actually came, the face screwed itself into an attitude of preparation for them.

"You can confer with me now?" Tertan said.

"Yes, I'd be glad to. There are several things in your two themes I want to talk to you about." Howe reached for the packet of themes on his desk and sought for Tertan's. But the boy was waving them away.

"These are done perforce," he said. "Under the pressure of your requirement. They are not significant, mere duties." Again his great hand flapped vaguely to dismiss his themes. He leaned forward and gazed at his teacher.

"You are," he said, "a man of letters? You are a poet?" It was more declaration than question.

"I should like to think so," Howe said.

At first Tertan accepted the answer with a show of appreciation, as though the understatement made a secret between himself and Howe. Then he chose to misunderstand. With his shrewd and disconcerting control of expression, he presented to Howe a puzzled grimace. "What does that mean?" he said.

Howe retracted the irony. "Yes. I am a poet." It sounded strange to say.

"That," Tertan said, "is a wonder." He corrected himself with his ducking head. "I mean that is wonderful."

Suddenly he dived at the miserable briefcase between his legs, put it on his knees and began to fumble with the catch, all intent on the difficulty it presented. Howe noted that his suit was worn thin, his shirt almost unclean. He became aware, even, of a vague and musty odor of garments worn too long in unaired rooms. Tertan conquered the lock and began to concentrate upon a search into the interior. At last he held in his hand what he was after, a torn and crumpled copy of *Life and Letters*.

"I learned it from here," he said, holding it out.

Howe looked at him sharply, his hackles a little up. But the boy's face was not only perfectly innocent, it even shone with a conscious admiration. Apparently nothing of the import of the essay had touched him except the wonderful fact that his teacher was a "man of letters." Yet this seemed too stupid and Howe, to test it, said, "The man who wrote that doesn't think it's wonderful."

Tertan made a moist hissing sound as he cleared his mouth of saliva. His head, oddly loose on his neck, wove a pattern of contempt in the air. "A critic," he said, "who admits *prima facie* that he does not understand." Then he said grandly, "It is the inevitable fate."

It was absurd, yet Howe was not only aware of the absurdity but of a tension suddenly and wonderfully relaxed. Now that the "attack" was on the table between himself and this strange boy and subject to the boy's funny and absolutely certain contempt, the hidden force of his feeling was revealed to him in the very moment that it vanished. All unsuspected, there had been a film over the world, a transparent but discoloring haze of danger. But he had no time to stop over the brightened aspect of things. Tertan was going on. "I also am a man of letters. Putative."

"You have written a good deal?" Howe meant to be no more than polite and he was surprised at the tenderness he heard in his words.

Solemnly the boy nodded, threw back the dank lock and sucked in a deep anticipatory breath. "First, a work of homiletics, which is a defense of the principles of religious optimism against the pessimism of Schopenhauer and the humanism of Nietzsche."

"Humanism? Why do you call it humanism?"

"It is my nomenclature for making a deity of man," Tertan replied negligently. "Then three fictional works, novels. And numerous essays in science, combating materialism. Is it your duty to read these if I bring them to you?"

Howe answered simply, "No, it isn't exactly my duty, but I shall be happy to read them."

Tertan stood up and remained silent. He rested his bag on the chair. With a certain compunction—for it did not seem entirely proper that, of two men of letters, one should have the right to blue-pencil the other, to grade him or to question the quality of his "sentence structure"—Howe reached for Tertan's papers. But before he could take them up, the boy suddenly made his bow-to-Abelard, the stiff inclination of the body with the hands seeming to emerge from the scholar's gown. Then he was gone.

But after his departure something was still left of him. The timbre of his curious sentences, the downright finality of so quaint a phrase as "It is the inevitable fate" still rang in the air. Howe gave the warmth of his feeling to the new visitor who stood at the door announcing himself with a genteel clearing of the throat.

"Dr. Howe, I believe?" the student said. A large hand advanced into the room and grasped Howe's hand. "Blackburn, sir, Theodore Blackburn, vice-president of the Student Council. A great pleasure, sir."

Out of a pair of ruddy cheeks a pair of small eyes twinkled good-naturedly. The large face, the large body were not so much fat as beefy and suggested something "typical," monk, politician, or innkeeper.

Blackburn took the seat beside Howe's desk. "I may have seemed to introduce myself in my public capacity, sir," he said. "But it is really as an individual that I came to see you. That is to say, as one of your students to be."

He spoke with an "English" intonation and he went on, "I was once an English major, sir."

For a moment Howe was startled, for the roast-beef look of the boy and the manner of his speech gave a second's credibility to one sense of his statement. Then the collegiate meaning of the phrase asserted itself, but some perversity made Howe say what was not really in good taste even with so forward a student, "Indeed? What regiment?"

Blackburn stared and then gave a little pouf-pouf of laughter. He waved the misapprehension away. *"Very* good, sir. It certainly is an ambiguous term." He chuckled in appreciation of Howe's joke, then cleared his throat to put it aside. "I look forward to taking your course in the romantic poets, sir," he said earnestly. "To me the romantic poets are the very crown of English literature."

Howe made a dry sound, and the boy, catching some meaning in it, said, "Little as I know them, of course. But even Shakespeare who is so dear to us of the Anglo-Saxon tradition is in a sense but the preparation for Shelley, Keats and Byron. And Wadsworth."

Almost sorry for him, Howe dropped his eyes. With some embarrassment, for the boy was not actually his student, he said softly, "Wordsworth."

"Sir?"

"Wordsworth, not Wadsworth. You said Wadsworth."

"Did I, sir?" Gravely he shook his head to rebuke himself for the error. "Wordsworth, of course—slip of the tongue." Then, quite in command again, he went on. "I have a favor to ask of you, Dr. Howe. You see, I began my college course as an English major,"—he smiled—"as I said."

"Yes?"

"But after my first year I shifted. I shifted to the social sciences. Sociology and government—I find them stimulating and very *real*." He paused, out of respect for reality. "But now I find that perhaps I have neglected the other side."

"The other side?" Howe said.

"Imagination, fancy, culture. A well-rounded man." He trailed off as if there were perfect understanding between them. "And so, sir, I have decided to end my senior year with your course in the romantic poets."

His voice was filled with an indulgence which Howe ignored as he said flatly and gravely, "But that course isn't given until the spring term."

"Yes, sir, and that is where the favor comes in. Would you let me take your romantic prose course? I can't take it for credit, sir, my program is full, but just for background it seems to me that I ought to take it. I do hope," he concluded in a manly way, "that you will consent."

"Well, it's no great favor, Mr. Blackburn. You can come if you wish, though there's not much point in it if you don't do the reading."

The bell rang for the hour and Howe got up.

"May I begin with this class, sir?" Blackburn's smile was candid and boyish.

Howe nodded carelessly and together, silently, they walked to the classroom down the hall. When they reached the door Howe stood back to let his student enter, but Blackburn moved adroitly behind him and grasped him by the arm to urge him over the threshold. They entered together with Blackburn's hand firmly on Howe's bicep, the student inducting the teacher into his own room. Howe felt a surge of temper rise in him and almost violently he disengaged his arm and walked to the desk, while Blackburn found a seat in the front row and smiled at him.

II

The question was, At whose door must the tragedy be laid?

All night the snow had fallen heavily and only now was abating in sparse little flurries. The windows were valanced high with white. It was very quiet, something of the quiet of the world had reached the class and Howe found that everyone was glad to talk or listen. In the room there was a comfortable sense of pleasure in being human.

Casebeer believed that the blame for the tragedy rested with heredity. Picking up the book he read, "The sins of the fathers are visited on their children." This opinion was received with general favor. Nevertheless Johnson ventured to say that the fault was all Pastor Manders' because the Pastor had made Mrs. Alving go back to her husband and was always hiding the truth. To this Hibbard objected with logic enough, "Well then, it was really all her husband's fault. He *did* all the bad things." De Witt, his face bright with an impatient idea, said that the fault was all society's. "By society I don't mean upper-crust society," he said. He looked around a little defiantly, taking in any members of the class who might be members of upper-crust society. "Not in that sense. I mean the social unit."

Howe nodded and said, "Yes, of course."

"If the society of the time had progressed far enough in science," De Witt went on, "then there would be no problem for Mr. Ibsen to write about. Captain Alving plays around a little, gives way to perfectly natural biological urges, and he gets a social disease, a venereal disease. If the disease is cured, no problem. Invent salvarsan and the disease is cured. The problem of heredity disappears and li'l Oswald just doesn't get paresis. No paresis, no problem—no problem, no play."

This was carrying the ark into battle and the class looked at De Witt with respectful curiosity. It was his usual way and on the whole they were sympathetic with his struggle to prove to Howe that science was better than literature. Still, there was something in his reckless manner that alienated them a little.

"Or take birth control, for instance," De Witt went on. "If Mrs. Alving had had some knowledge of contraception, she wouldn't have had to have li'l Oswald at all. No li'l Oswald, no play."

The class was suddenly quieter. In the back row Stettenhover swung his great football shoulders in a righteous sulking gesture, first to the right, then to the left. He puckered his mouth ostentatiously. Intellect was always ending up by talking dirty.

Tertan's hand went up and Howe said, "Mr. Tertan." The boy shambled to his feet and began his long characteristic gulp. Howe made a motion with his fingers, as small as possible, and Tertan ducked his head and smiled in apology. He sat down. The class laughed. With more than half the term gone, Tertan had not been able to remember that one did not rise to speak. He seemed unable to carry on the life of the intellect without this mark of respect for it. To Howe the boy's habit of rising seemed to accord with the formal shabbiness of his dress. He never wore the casual sweaters and jackets of his classmates. Into the free and comfortable air of the college classroom he brought the stuffy sordid strictness of some crowded metropolitan high school.

"Speaking from one sense," Tertan began slowly, "there is no blame ascribable. From the sense of determinism, who can say where the blame lies? The preordained is the preordained and it cannot be said without rebellion against the universe, a palpable absurdity."

In the back row Stettenhover slumped suddenly in his seat, his heels held out before him, making a loud dry disgusted sound. His body sank until his neck rested on the back of his chair. He folded his hands across his belly and looked significantly out of the window, exasperated not only with Tertan but with Howe, with the class, with the whole system designed to encourage this kind of thing. There was a certain insolence in the movement and Howe flushed. As Tertan continued to speak, Howe walked casually toward the window and placed himself in the line of Stettenhover's vision. He stared at the great fellow, who pretended not to see him. There was so much power in the big body, so much contempt in the Greek-athlete face under the crisp Greek-athlete curls, that Howe felt almost physical fear. But at last Stettenhover admitted him to focus and under his disapproving gaze sat up with slow indifference. His eyebrows raised high in resignation, he began to examine his hands. Howe relaxed and turned his attention back to Tertan.

"Flux of existence," Tertan was saying, "produces all things, so that judgment wavers. Beyond the phenomena, what? But phenomena are adumbrated and to them we are limited."

Howe saw it for a moment as perhaps it existed in the boy's mind —the world of shadows which are cast by a great light upon a hidden reality as in the old myth of the Cave. But the little brush with Stettenhover had tired him and he said irritably, "But come to the point, Mr. Tertan."

He said it so sharply that some of the class looked at him curiously. For three months he had gently carried Tertan through his verbosities, to the vaguely respectful surprise of the other students, who seemed to conceive that there existed between this strange classmate and their teacher some special understanding from which they were content to be excluded. Tertan looked at him mildly and at once came brilliantly to the point. "This is the summation of the play," he said and took up his book and read, " 'Your poor father never found any outlet for the overmastering joy of life that was in him. And I brought no holiday into his home, either. Everything seemed to turn upon duty and I am afraid I made your poor father's home unbearable to him, Oswald.' Spoken by Mrs. Alving."

Yes, that was surely the "summation" of the play and Tertan had hit it, as he hit, deviously and eventually, the literary point of almost everything. But now, as always, he was wrapping it away from sight. "For most mortals," he said, "there are only joys of biological urgings, gross and crass, such as the sensuous Captain Alving. For certain few there are the transmutations beyond these to a contemplation of the utter whole."

Oh, the boy was mad. And suddenly the word, used in hyperbole, intended almost for the expression of exasperated admiration, became literal. Now that the word was used, it became simply apparent to Howe that Tertan was mad.

It was a monstrous word and stood like a bestial thing in the room. Yet it so completely comprehended everything that had puzzled Howe, it so arranged and explained what for three months had been perplexing him that almost at once its horror became domesticated. With this word Howe was able to understand why he had never been able to communicate to Tertan the value of a single criticism or correction of his wild, verbose themes. Their conferences had been frequent and long but had done nothing to reduce to order the splendid confusion of the boy's ideas. Yet, impossible though its expression was, Tertan's incandescent mind could always strike for a moment into some dark corner of thought.

And now it was suddenly apparent that it was not a faulty rhetoric that Howe had to contend with. With his new knowledge he looked at Tertan's face and wondered how he could have so long deceived himself. Tertan was still talking and the class had lapsed into a kind of patient unconsciousness, a coma of respect for words which, for all that most of them knew, might be profound. Almost with a suffusion of shame, Howe believed that in some dim way the class had long ago had some intimation of Tertan's madness. He reached out as decisively as he could to seize the thread of Tertan's discourse before it should be entangled further.

"Mr. Tertan says that the blame must be put upon whoever kills the joy of living in another. We have been assuming that Captain Alving was a wholly bad man, but what if we assume that he became bad only because Mrs. Alving, when they were first married, acted toward him in the prudish way she says she did?"

It was a ticklish idea to advance to freshmen and perhaps not profitable. Not all of them were following.

"That would put the blame on Mrs. Alving herself, whom most of you admire. And she herself seems to think so." He glanced at his watch. The hour was nearly over. "What do you think, Mr. De Witt?"

De Witt rose to the idea, wanted to know if society couldn't be blamed for educating Mrs. Alving's temperament in the wrong way. Casebeer was puzzled, Stettenhover continued to look at his hands until the bell rang.

Tertan, his brows louring in thought, was making as always for a private word. Howe gathered his books and papers to leave quickly. At this moment of his discovery and with the knowledge still raw, he could not engage himself with Tertan. Tertan sucked in his breath to prepare for speech and Howe made ready for the pain and confusion. But at that moment Casebeer detached himself from the group with which he had been conferring and which he seemed to represent. His constituency remained at a tactful distance. The mission involved the time of an assigned essay. Casebeer's presentation of the plea—it was based on the freshmen's heavy duties at the fraternities during Carnival Week—cut across Tertan's preparations for speech. "And so some of us fellows thought," Casebeer concluded with heavy solemnity, "that we could do a better job, give our minds to it more, if we had more time."

Tertan regarded Casebeer with mingled curiosity and revulsion. Howe not only said that he would postpone the assignment but went on to talk about the Carnival and even drew the waiting constituency into the conversation. He was conscious of Tertan's stern and astonished stare, then of his sudden departure.

Now that the fact was clear, Howe knew that he must act on it. His course was simple enough. He must lay the case before the Dean. Yet he hesitated. His feeling for Tertan must now, certainly, be in some way invalidated. Yet could he, because of a word, hurry to assign to official and reasonable solicitude what had been, until this moment, so various and warm? He could at least delay and, by moving slowly, lend a poor grace to the necessary, ugly act of making his report.

It was with some notion of keeping the matter in his own hands that he went to the Dean's office to look up Tertan's records. In the outer office the Dean's secretary greeted him brightly and at his request brought him the manila folder with the small identifying photograph pasted in the corner. She laughed. "He was looking for the birdie in the wrong place," she said.

Howe leaned over her shoulder to look at the picture. It was as bad as all the Dean's-office photographs were, but it differed from all that Howe had ever seen. Tertan, instead of looking into the camera, as no doubt he had been bidden, had, at the moment of exposure, turned his eyes upward. His mouth, as though conscious of the trick played on the photographer, had the sly superior look that Howe knew.

The secretary was fascinated by the picture. "What a funny boy," she said. "He looks like Tartuffe!"

And so he did, with the absurd piety of the eyes and the conscious slyness of the mouth and the whole face bloated by the bad lens.

"Is he *like* that?" the secretary said.

"Like Tartuffe? No."

From the photograph there was little enough comfort to be had. The records themselves gave no clue to madness, though they suggested sadness enough. Howe read of a father, Stanislaus Tertan, born in Budapest and trained in engineering in Berlin, once employed by the Hercules Chemical Corporation—this was one of the factories that dominated the south end of the town—but now without employment. He read of a mother Erminie (Youngfellow) Tertan, born in Manchester, educated at a Normal School at Leeds, now housewife by profession. The family lived on Greenbriar Street, which Howe knew as a row of once elegant homes near what was now the factory district. The old mansions had long ago been divided into small and primitive apartments. Of Ferdinand himself there was little to learn. He lived with his parents, had attended a Detroit high school and had transferred to the local school in his last year. His rating for intelligence, as expressed in numbers, was high, his scholastic record was remarkable, he held a college scholarship for his tuition.

Howe laid the folder on the secretary's desk. "Did you find what you wanted to know?" she asked.

The phrases from Tertan's momentous first theme came back to him. "Tertan I am, but what is Tertan? Of this time, of that place, of some parentage, what does it matter?"

"No, I didn't find it," he said.

Now that he had consulted the sad half-meaningless record he knew all the more firmly that he must not give the matter out of his own hands. He must not release Tertan to authority. Not that he anticipated from the Dean anything but the greatest kindness for Tertan. The Dean would have the experience and skill which he himself could not have. One way or another the Dean could answer the question, "What is Tertan?" Yet this was precisely what he feared. He alone could keep alive—not forever but for a somehow important time—the question, "What is Tertan?" He alone could keep it still a question. Some sure instinct told him that he must not surrender the question to a clean official desk in a clear official light to be dealt with, settled and closed.

He heard himself saying, "Is the Dean busy at the moment? I'd like to see him."

His request came thus unbidden, even forbidden, and it was one of the surprising and startling incidents of his life. Later, when he reviewed the events, so disconnected in themselves or so merely odd, of the story that unfolded for him that year, it was over this moment, on its face the least notable, that he paused longest. It was frequently to be with fear and never without a certainty of its meaning in his own knowledge of himself that he would recall this simple, routine request and the feeling of shame and freedom it gave him as he sent everything down the official chute. In the end, of course, no matter what he did to "protect" Tertan, he would have had to make the same request and lay the matter on the Dean's clean desk. But it would always be a landmark of his life that, at the very moment when he was rejecting the official way, he had been, without will or intention, so gladly drawn to it.

After the storm's last delicate flurry, the sun had come out. Reflected by the new snow, it filled the office with a golden light which was almost musical in the way it made all the commonplace objects of efficiency shine with a sudden sad and noble significance. And the light, now that he noticed it, made the utterance of his perverse and unwanted request even more momentous.

The secretary consulted the engagement pad. "He'll be free any minute. Don't you want to wait in the parlor?"

She threw open the door of the large and pleasant room in which the Dean held his Committee meetings and in which his visitors waited. It was designed with a homely elegance on the masculine side of the eighteenth-century manner. There was a small coal fire in the grate and the handsome mahogany table was strewn with books and magazines. The large windows gave on the snowy lawn and there was such a fine width of window that the white casements and walls seemed at this moment but a continuation of the snow, the snow but an extension of casement and walls. The outdoors seemed taken in and made safe, the indoors seemed luxuriously freshened and expanded.

Howe sat down by the fire and lighted a cigarette. The room had its intended effect upon him. He felt comfortable and relaxed, yet nicely organized, some young diplomatic agent of the eighteenth century, the newly fledged Swift carrying out Sir William Temple's business. The rawness of Tertan's case quite vanished. He crossed his legs and reached for a magazine.

It was that famous issue of *Life and Letters* that his idle hand had found and his blood raced as he sifted through it and the shape of his own name, Joseph Howe, sprang out at him, still cabalistic in its power. He tossed the magazine back on the table as the door of the Dean's office opened and the Dean ushered out Theodore Blackburn.

"Ah, Joseph!" the Dean said.

Blackburn said, "Good morning, Doctor." Howe winced at the title and caught the flicker of amusement over the Dean's face. The Dean stood with his hand high on the doorjamb and Blackburn, still in the doorway, remained standing almost under his long arm.

Howe nodded briefly to Blackburn, snubbing his eager deference. "Can you give me a few minutes?" he said to the Dean.

"All the time you want. Come in." Before the two men could enter the office, Blackburn claimed their attention with a long full "Er." As they turned to him, Blackburn said, "Can *you* give *me* a few minutes, Dr. Howe?" His eyes sparkled at the little audacity he had committed, the slightly impudent play with hierarchy. Of the three of them Blackburn kept himself the lowest, but he reminded Howe of his subaltern relation to the Dean.

"I mean, of course," Blackburn went on easily, "when you've finished with the Dean."

"I'll be in my office shortly," Howe said, turned his back on the ready "Thank you, sir," and followed the Dean into the inner room.

"Energetic boy," said the Dean. "A bit beyond himself but very energetic. Sit down."

The Dean lighted a cigarette, leaned back in his chair, sat easy and silent for a moment, giving Howe no signal to go ahead with business. He was a young Dean, not much beyond forty, a tall handsome man with sad, ambitious eyes. He had been a Rhodes scholar. His friends looked for great things from him and it was generally said that he had notions of education which he was not yet ready to try to put into practice.

His relaxed silence was meant as a compliment to Howe. He smiled and said, "What's the business, Joseph?"

"Do you know Tertan—Ferdinand Tertan, a freshman?"

The Dean's cigarette was in his mouth and his hands were clasped behind his head. He did not seem to search his memory for the name. He said, "What about him?"

Clearly the Dean knew something and he was waiting for Howe to tell him more. Howe moved only tentatively. Now that he was doing what he resolved not to do, he felt more guilty at having been so long deceived by Tertan and more need to be loyal to his error.

"He's a strange fellow," he ventured. He said stubbornly, "In a strange way he's very brilliant." He concluded, "But very strange."

The springs of the Dean's swivel chair creaked as he came out of his sprawl and leaned forward to Howe. "Do you mean he's so strange that it's something you could give a name to?"

Howe looked at him stupidly. "What do you mean?" he said.

"What's his trouble?" the Dean said more neutrally.

"He's very brilliant, in a way. I looked him up and he has a top intelligence rating. But somehow, and it's hard to explain just how, what he says is always on the edge of sense and doesn't quite make it."

The Dean looked at him and Howe flushed up. The Dean had surely read Woolley on the subject of "the Howes" and the *tour d'ivresse*. Was that quick glance ironical?

The Dean picked up some papers from his desk and Howe could see that they were in Tertan's impatient scrawl. Perhaps the little gleam in the Dean's glance had come only from putting facts together.

"He sent me this yesterday," the Dean said. "After an interview I had with him. I haven't been able to do more than glance at it. When you said what you did, I realized there was something wrong."

Twisting his mouth, the Dean looked over the letter. "You seem to be involved," he said without looking up. "By the way, what did you give him at midterm?"

Flushing, setting his shoulders, Howe said firmly, "I gave him A-minus."

The Dean chuckled. "Might be a good idea if some of our boys went crazy—just a little." He said, "Well," to conclude the matter and handed the papers to Howe. "See if this is the same thing you've been finding. Then we can go into the matter again."

Before the fire in the parlor, in the chair that Howe had been occupying, sat Blackburn. He sprang to his feet as Howe entered.

"I said my office, Mr. Blackburn." Howe's voice was sharp. Then he was almost sorry for the rebuke, so clearly and naively did Blackburn seem to relish his stay in the parlor, close to authority.

"I'm in a bit of a hurry, sir," he said, "and I did want to be sure to speak to you, sir."

He was really absurd, yet fifteen years from now he would have grown up to himself, to the assurance and mature beefiness. In banks, in consular offices, in brokerage firms, on the bench, more seriously affable, a little sterner, he would make use of his ability to be administered by his job. It was almost reassuring. Now he was exercising his too-great skill on Howe. "I owe you an apology, sir," he said.

Howe knew that he did but he showed surprise.

"I mean, Doctor, after you having been so kind about letting me attend your class, I stopped coming." He smiled in deprecation. "Extra-curricular activities take up so much of my time. I'm afraid I undertook more than I could perform."

Howe had noticed the absence and had been a little irritated by it after Blackburn's elaborate plea. It was an absence that might be interpreted as a comment on the teacher. But there was only one way for him to answer. "You've no need to apologize," he said. "It's wholly your affair."

Blackburn beamed. "I'm so glad you feel that way about it, sir. I was worried you might think I had stayed away because I was influenced by—" He stopped and lowered his eyes.

Astonished, Howe said, "Influenced by what?"

"Well, by—" Blackburn hesitated and for answer pointed to the table on which lay the copy of *Life and Letters*. Without looking at it, he knew where to direct his hand. "By the unfavorable publicity, sir." He hurried on. "And that brings me to another point, sir. I am secretary of Quill and Scroll, sir, the student literary society, and I wonder if you would address us. You could read your own poetry, sir, and defend your own point of view. It would be very interesting."

It was truly amazing. Howe looked long and cruelly into Blackburn's face, trying to catch the secret of the mind that could have conceived this way of manipulating him, this way so daring and inept—but not entirely inept—with its malice so without malignity. The face did not yield its secret. Howe smiled broadly and said, "Of course I don't think you were influenced by the unfavorable publicity."

"I'm still going to take—regularly, for credit—your romantic poets course next term," Blackburn said.

"Don't worry, my dear fellow, don't worry about it."

Howe started to leave and Blackburn stopped him with, "But about Quill, sir?"

"Suppose we wait until next term? I'll be less busy then."

And Blackburn said, "Very good, sir, and thank you."

In his office the little encounter seemed less funny to Howe, was even in some indeterminate way disturbing. He made an effort to put it from his mind by turning to what was sure to disturb him more, the Tertan letter read in the new interpretation. He found what he had always found, the same florid leaps beyond fact and meaning, the same headlong certainty. But as his eye passed over the familiar scrawl it caught his own name and for the second time that hour he felt the race of his blood.

"The Paraclete," Tertan had written to the Dean, "from a Greek word meaning to stand in place of, but going beyond the primitive idea to mean traditionally the helper, the one who comforts and assists, cannot without fundamental loss be jettisoned. Even if taken no longer in the supernatural case, the concept remains deeply in the human consciousness inevitably. Humanitarianism is no reply, for not every man stands in the place of every other man for this other's comrade comfort. But certain are chosen out of the human race to be the consoler of some other. Of these, for example, is Joseph Barker Howe, Ph.D. Of intellects not the first yet of true intellect and lambent instructions, given to that which is intuitive and irrational, not to what is logical in the strict word, what is judged by him is of the heart and not the head. Here is one chosen, in that he chooses himself to stand in the place of another for comfort and consolation. To him more than another I give my gratitude, with all respect to our Dean who reads this, a noble man, but merely dedicated, not consecrated. But not in the aspect of the Paraclete only is Dr. Joseph Barker Howe established, for he must be the Paraclete to another aspect of himself, that which is driven and persecuted by the lack of understanding in the world at large, so that he in himself embodies the full history of man's tribulations and, overflowing upon others, notably the present writer, is the ultimate end."

This was love. There was no escape from it. Try as Howe might to remember that Tertan was mad and all his emotions invalidated, he could not destroy the effect upon him of his student's stern, affectionate regard. He had betrayed not only a power of mind but a power of love. And however firmly he held before his attention the fact of Tertan's madness, he could do nothing to banish the physical sensation of gratitude he felt. He had never thought of himself as "driven and persecuted" and he did not now. But still he could not make meaningless his sensation of gratitude. The pitiable Tertan sternly pitied him, and comfort came from Tertan's never-to-be comforted mind.

III

In an academic community, even an efficient one, official matters move slowly. The term drew to a close with no action in the case of Tertan, and Joseph Howe had to confront a curious problem. How should he grade his strange student, Tertan?

Tertan's final examination had been no different from all his other writing, and what did one "give" such a student? De Witt must have his A, that was clear. Johnson would get a B. With Casebeer it was a question of a B-minus or a C-plus, and Stettenhover, who had been crammed by the team tutor to fill half a blue-book with his thin feminine scrawl, would have his C-minus which he would accept with mingled indifference and resentment. But with Tertan it was not so easy.

The boy was still in the college process and his name could not be omitted from the grade sheet. Yet what should a mind under suspicion of madness be graded? Until the medical verdict was given, it was for Howe to continue as Tertan's teacher and to keep his judgment pedagogical. Impossible to give him an F: he had not failed. B was for Johnson's stolid mediocrity. He could not be put on the edge of passing with Stettenhover, for he exactly did not pass. In energy and richness of intellect he was perhaps even De Witt's superior, and Howe toyed grimly with the notion of giving him an A, but that would lower the value of the A De Witt had won with his beautiful and clear, if still arrogant, mind. There was a notation which the Registrar recognized—Inc. for Incomplete and in the horrible comedy of the situation, Howe considered that. But really only a mark of M. for Mad would serve.

In his perplexity, Howe sought the Dean, but the Dean was out of town. In the end, he decided to maintain the A-minus he had given Tertan at midterm. After all, there had been no falling away from that quality. He entered it on the grade sheet with something like bravado.

Academic time moves quickly. A college year is not really a year, lacking as it does three months. And it is endlessly divided into units which, at their beginning, appear larger than they are—terms, half-terms, months, weeks. And the ultimate unit, the hour, is not really an hour, lacking as it does ten minutes. And so the new term advanced rapidly and one day the fields about the town were all brown, cleared of even the few thin patches of snow which had lingered so long.

Howe, as he lectured on the romantic poets, became conscious of Blackburn emanating wrath. Blackburn did it well, did it with enormous dignity. He did not stir in his seat, he kept his eyes fixed on Howe in perfect attention, but he abstained from using his notebook, there was no mistaking what he proposed to himself as an attitude. His elbow on the writing-wing of the chair, his chin on the curled fingers of his hand, he was the embodiment of intellectual indignation. He was thinking his own thoughts, would give no public offense, yet would claim his due, was not to be intimidated. Howe knew that he would present himself at the end of the hour.

Blackburn entered the office without invitation. He did not smile, there was no cajolery about him. Without invitation he sat down beside Howe's desk. He did not speak until he had taken the blue-book from his pocket. He said, "What does this mean, sir?"

It was a sound and conservative student tactic. Said in the usual way it meant, "How could you have so misunderstood me?" or "What does this mean for my future in the course?" But there were none of the humbler tones in Blackburn's way of saying it.

Howe made the established reply, "I think that's for you to tell me."

Blackburn continued icy. "I'm sure I can't, sir."

There was a silence between them. Both dropped their eyes to the blue-book on the desk. On its cover Howe had penciled: "F. This is very poor work."

Howe picked up the blue-book. There was always the possibility of injustice. The teacher may be bored by the mass of papers and not wholly attentive. A phrase, even the student's handwriting, may irritate him unreasonably. "Well," said Howe, "let's go through it."

He opened the first page. "Now here: you write, 'In *The Ancient Mariner,* Coleridge lives in and transports us to a honey-sweet world where all is rich and strange, a world of charm to which we can escape from the humdrum existence of our daily lives, the world of romance. Here, in this warm and honey-sweet land of charming dreams we can relax and enjoy ourselves.'"

Howe lowered the paper and waited with a neutral look for Blackburn to speak. Blackburn returned the look boldly, did not speak, sat stolid and lofty. At last Howe said, speaking gently, "Did you mean that, or were you just at a loss for something to say?"

"You imply that I was just 'bluffing'?" The quotation marks hung palpable in the air about the word.

"I'd like to know. I'd prefer believing that you were bluffing to believing that you really thought this."

Blackburn's eyebrows went up. From the height of a great and firm-based idea he looked at his teacher. He clasped the crags for a moment and then pounced, craftily, suavely. "Do you mean, Dr. Howe, that there aren't two opinions possible?"

It was superbly done in its air of putting all of Howe's intellectual life into the balance. Howe remained patient and simple. "Yes, many opinions are possible, but not this one. Whatever anyone believes of *The Ancient Mariner,* no one can in reason believe that it represents a—a honey-sweet world in which we can relax."

"But that is what I *feel,* sir."

This was well done too. Howe said, "Look, Mr. Blackburn. Do you really relax with hunger and thirst, the heat and the sea-serpents, the dead men with staring eyes, Life in Death and the skeletons? Come now, Mr. Blackburn."

Blackburn made no answer and Howe pressed forward. "Now you say of Wordsworth, 'Of peasant stock himself, he turned from the effete life of the salons and found in the peasant the hope of a flaming revolution which would sweep away all the old ideas. This is the subject of his best poems.'"

Beaming at his teacher with youthful eagerness, Blackburn said, "Yes, sir, a rebel, a bringer of light to suffering mankind. I see him as a kind of Prothemeus."

"A kind of what?"

"Prothemeus, sir."

"Think, Mr. Blackburn. We were talking about him only today and I mentioned his name a dozen times. You don't mean Prothemeus. You mean—" Howe waited but there was no response.

"You mean Prometheus."

Blackburn gave no assent and Howe took the reins. "You've done a bad job here, Mr. Blackburn, about as bad as could be done." He saw Blackburn stiffen and his genial face harden again. "It shows either a lack of preparation or a complete lack of understanding." He saw Blackburn's face begin to go to pieces and he stopped.

"Oh, sir," Blackburn burst out, "I've never had a mark like this before, never anything below a B, never. A thing like this has never happened to me before."

It must be true, it was a statement too easily verified. Could it be that other instructors accepted such flaunting nonsense? Howe wanted to end the interview. "I'll set it down to lack of preparation," he said. "I know you're busy. That's not an excuse but it's an explanation. Now suppose you really prepare and then take another quiz in two weeks. We'll forget this one and count the other."

Blackburn squirmed with pleasure and gratitude. "Thank you, sir. You're really very kind, very kind."

Howe rose to conclude the visit. "All right then—in two weeks."

It was that day that the Dean imparted to Howe the conclusion of the case of Tertan. It was simple and a little anticlimactic. A physician had been called in, and had said the word, given the name.

"A classic case, he called it," the Dean said. "Not a doubt in the world," he said. His eyes were full of miserable pity and he clutched at a word. "A classic case, a classic case." To his aid and to Howe's there came the Parthenon and the form of the Greek drama, the Aristotelian logic, Racine and the Well-Tempered Clavichord, the blueness of the Aegean and its clear sky. Classic— that is to say, without a doubt, perfect in its way, a veritable model, and, as the Dean had been told, sure to take a perfectly predictable and inevitable course to a foreknown conclusion.

It was not only pity that stood in the Dean's eyes. For a moment there was fear too. "Terrible," he said, "it is simply terrible."

Then he went on briskly. "Naturally we've told the boy nothing. And naturally we won't. His tuition's paid by his scholarship and we'll continue him on the rolls until the end of the year. That will be kindest. After that the matter will be out of our control. We'll see, of course, that he gets into the proper hands. I'm told there will be no change, he'll go on like this, be as good as this, for four to six months. And so we'll just go along as usual."

So Tertan continued to sit in Section 5 of English 1A, to his classmates still a figure of curiously dignified fun, symbol to most of them of the respectable but absurd intellectual life. But to his teacher he was now very different. He had not changed—he was still the greyhound casting for the scent of ideas and Howe could see that he was still the same Tertan, but he could not feel it. What he felt as he looked at the boy sitting in his accustomed place was the hard blank of a fact. The fact itself was formidable and depressing. But what Howe was chiefly aware of was that he had permitted the metamorphosis of Tertan from person to fact.

As much as possible he avoided seeing Tertan's upraised hand and eager eye. But the fact did not know of its mere factuality, it continued its existence as if it were Tertan, hand up and eye questioning, and one day it appeared in Howe's office with a document.

"Even the spirit who lives egregiously, above the herd, must have its relations with the fellowman," Tertan declared. He laid the document on Howe's desk. It was headed "Quill and Scroll Society of Dwight College. Application for Membership."

"In most ways these are crass minds," Tertan said, touching the paper. "Yet as a whole, bound together in their common love of letters, they transcend their intellectual lacks, since it is not a paradox that the whole is greater than the sum of its parts."

"When are the elections?" Howe asked.

"They take place tomorrow."

"I certainly hope you will be successful."

"Thank you. Would you wish to implement that hope?" A rather dirty finger pointed to the bottom of the sheet. "A faculty recommender is necessary," Tertan said stiffly, and waited.

"And you wish me to recommend you?"

"It would be an honor."

"You may use my name."

Tertan's finger pointed again. "It must be a written sponsorship, signed by the sponsor." There was a large blank space on the form under the heading, "Opinion of Faculty Sponsor."

This was almost another thing and Howe hesitated. Yet there was nothing else to do and he took out his fountain pen. He wrote, "Mr. Ferdinand Tertan is marked by his intense devotion to letters and by his exceptional love of all things of the mind." To this he signed his name which looked bold and assertive on the white page. It disturbed him, the strange affirming power of a name. With a businesslike air, Tertan whipped up the paper, folded it with decision and put it into his pocket. He bowed and took his departure, leaving Howe with the sense of having done something oddly momentous.

And so much now seemed odd and momentous to Howe that should not have seemed so. It was odd and momentous, he felt, when he sat with Blackburn's second quiz before him and wrote in an excessively firm hand the grade of C-minus. The paper was a clear, an indisputable failure. He was carefully and consciously committing a cowardice. Blackburn had told the truth when he had pleaded his past record. Howe had consulted it in the Dean's office. It showed no grade lower than a B-minus. A canvass of some of Blackburn's previous instructors had brought vague attestations to the adequate powers of a student imperfectly remembered and sometimes surprise that his abilities could be questioned at all.

As he wrote the grade, Howe told himself that this cowardice sprang from an unwillingness to have more dealings with a student he disliked. He knew it was simpler than that. He knew he feared Blackburn: that was the absurd truth. And cowardice did not solve the matter after all. Blackburn, flushed with a first success, attacked at once. The minimal passing grade had not assuaged his feelings and he sat at Howe's desk and again the blue-book lay between them. Blackburn said nothing. With an enormous impudence, he was waiting for Howe to speak and explain himself.

At last Howe said sharply and rudely, "Well?" His throat was tense and the blood was hammering in his head. His mouth was tight with anger at himself for his disturbance.

Blackburn's glance was almost baleful. "This is impossible, sir."

"But there it is," Howe answered.

"Sir?" Blackburn had not caught the meaning but his tone was still haughty.

Impatiently Howe said, "There it is, plain as day. Are you here to complain again?"

"Indeed I am, sir." There was surprise in Blackburn's voice that Howe should ask the question.

"I shouldn't complain if I were you. You did a thoroughly bad job on your first quiz. This one is a little, only a very little, better." This was not true. If anything, it was worse.

"That might be a matter of opinion, sir."

"It is a matter of opinion. Of my opinion."

"Another opinion might be different, sir."

"You really believe that?" Howe said.

"Yes." The omission of the "sir" was monumental.

"Whose, for example?"

"The Dean's, for example." Then the fleshy jaw came forward a little. "Or a certain literary critic's, for example."

It was colossal and almost too much for Blackburn himself to handle. The solidity of his face almost crumpled under it. But he withstood his own audacity and went on. "And the Dean's opinion might be guided by the knowledge that the person who gave me this mark is the man whom a famous critic, the most eminent judge of literature in this country, called a drunken man. The Dean might think twice about whether such a man is fit to teach Dwight students."

Howe said in quiet admonition, "Blackburn, you're mad," meaning no more than to check the boy's extravagance.

But Blackburn paid no heed. He had another shot in the locker. "And the Dean might be guided by the information, of which I have evidence, documentary evidence,"—he slapped his breast pocket twice—"that this same person personally recommended to the college literary society, the oldest in the country, that he personally recommended a student who is crazy, who threw the meeting into an uproar, a psychiatric case. The Dean might take that into account."

Howe was never to learn the details of that "uproar." He had always to content himself with the dim but passionate picture which at that moment sprang into his mind, of Tertan standing on some abstract height and madly denouncing the multitude of Quill and Scroll who howled him down.

He sat quiet a moment and looked at Blackburn. The ferocity had entirely gone from the student's face. He sat regarding his teacher almost benevolently. He had played a good card and now, scarcely at all unfriendly, he was waiting to see the effect. Howe took up the blue-book and negligently sifted through it. He read a page, closed the book, struck out the C-minus and wrote an F.

"Now you may take the paper to the Dean," he said. "You may tell him that after reconsidering it, I lowered the grade."

The gasp was audible. "Oh sir!" Blackburn cried. "Please!" His face was agonized. "It means my graduation, my livelihood, my future. Don't do this to me."

"It's done already."

Blackburn stood up. "I spoke rashly, sir, hastily. I had no intention, no real intention, of seeing the Dean. It rests with you—entirely, entirely. I *hope* you will restore the first mark."

"Take the matter to the Dean or not, just as you choose. The grade is what you deserve and it stands."

Blackburn's head dropped. "And will I be failed at mid-term, sir?"

"Of course."

From deep out of Blackburn's great chest rose a cry of anguish. "Oh sir, if you want me to go down on my knees to you, I will, I will."

Howe looked at him in amazement.

"I will, I will. On my knees, sir. This mustn't, mustn't happen."

He spoke so literally, meaning so very truly that his knees and exactly his knees were involved and seeming to think that he was offering something of tangible value to his teacher, that Howe, whose head had become icy clear in the nonsensical drama, thought, "The boy is mad," and began to speculate fantastically whether something in himself attracted or developed aberration. He could see himself standing absurdly before the Dean and saying, "I've found another. This time it's the vice-president of the Council, the manager of the debating team, and secretary of Quill and Scroll."

One more such discovery, he thought, and he himself would be discovered! And there, suddenly, Blackburn was on his knees with a thump, his huge thighs straining his trousers, his hands outstretched in a great gesture of supplication.

With a cry, Howe shoved back his swivel chair and it rolled away on its casters half across the little room. Blackburn knelt for a moment to nothing at all, then got to his feet.

Howe rose abruptly. He said, "Blackburn, you will stop acting like an idiot. Dust your knees off, take your paper and get out.

You've behaved like a fool and a malicious person. You have half a term to do a decent job. Keep your silly mouth shut and try to do it. Now get out."

Blackburn's head was low. He raised it and there was a pious light in his eyes. "Will you shake hands, sir?" he said. He thrust out his hand.

"I will not," Howe said.

Head and hand sank together. Blackburn picked up his blue-book and walked to the door. He turned and said, "Thank you, sir." His back, as he departed, was heavy with tragedy and stateliness.

IV

After years of bad luck with the weather, the College had a perfect day for Commencement. It was wonderfully bright, the air so transparent, the wind so brisk that no one could resist talking about it.

As Howe set out for the campus he heard Hilda calling from the back yard. She called, "Professor, professor," and came running to him.

Howe said, "What's this 'professor' business?"

"Mother told me," Hilda said. "You've been promoted. And I want to take your picture."

"Next year," said Howe. "I won't be a professor until next year. And you know better than to call anybody 'professor.'"

"It was just in fun," Hilda said. She seemed disappointed.

"But you can take my picture if you want. I won't look much different next year." Still, it was frightening. It might mean that he was to stay in this town all his life.

Hilda brightened. "Can I take it in this?" she said, and touched the gown he carried over his arm.

Howe laughed. "Yes, you can take it in this."

"I'll get my things and meet you in front of Otis," Hilda said. "I have the background all picked out."

On the campus the Commencement crowd was already large. It stood about in eager, nervous little family groups. As he crossed, Howe was greeted by a student, capped and gowned, glad of the chance to make an event for his parents by introducing one of his teachers. It was while Howe stood there chatting that he saw Tertan.

He had never seen anyone quite so alone, as though a circle had been woven about him to separate him from the gay crowd on the campus. Not that Tertan was not gay, he was the gayest of all. Three weeks had passed since Howe had last seen him, the weeks of examination, the lazy week before Commencement, and this was now a different Tertan. On his head he wore a panama hat, broad-brimmed and fine, of the shape associated with South American planters. He wore a suit of raw silk, luxurious but yellowed with age and much too tight, and he sported a whangee cane. He walked sedately, the hat tilted at a devastating angle, the stick coming up and down in time to his measured tread. He had, Howe guessed, outfitted himself to greet the day in the clothes of that ruined father whose existence was on record in the Dean's office. Gravely and arrogantly he surveyed the scene—in it, his whole bearing seemed to say, but not of it. With his haughty step, with his flashing eye, Tertan was coming nearer. Howe did not wish to be seen. He shifted his position slightly. When he looked again, Tertan was not in sight.

The chapel clock struck the quarter hour. Howe detached himself from his chat and hurried to Otis Hall at the far end of the campus. Hilda had not yet come. He went up into the high portico and, using the glass of the door for a mirror, put on his gown, adjusted the hood on his shoulders and set the mortarboard on his head. When he came down the steps Hilda had arrived.

Nothing could have told him more forcibly that a year had

passed than the development of Hilda's photographic possessions from the box camera of the previous fall. By a strap about her neck was hung a leather case, so thick and strong, so carefully stitched and so molded to its contents that it could only hold a costly camera. The appearance was deceptive, Howe knew, for he had been present at the Aikens' pre-Christmas conference about its purchase. It was only a fairly good domestic camera. Still, it looked very impressive. Hilda carried another leather case from which she drew a collapsible tripod. Decisively she extended each of its gleaming legs and set it up on the path. She removed the camera from its case and fixed it to the tripod. In its compact efficiency the camera almost had a life of its own, but Hilda treated it with easy familiarity, looked into its eye, glanced casually at its gauges. Then from a pocket she took still another leather case and drew from it a small instrument through which she looked first at Howe, who began to feel inanimate and lost, and then at the sky. She made some adjustment on the instrument, then some adjustment on the camera. She swept the scene with her eye, found a spot and pointed the camera in its direction. She walked to the spot, stood on it and beckoned to Howe. With each new leather case, with each new instrument and with each new adjustment she had grown in ease and now she said, "Joe, will you stand here?"

Obediently Howe stood where he was bidden. She had yet another instrument. She took out a tape-measure on a mechanical spool. Kneeling down before Howe, she put the little metal ring of the tape under the tip of his shoe. At her request, Howe pressed it with his toe. When she had measured her distance, she nodded to Howe who released the tape. At a touch, it sprang back into the spool. "You have to be careful if you're going to get what you want," Hilda said. "I don't believe in all this snap-snap-snapping," she remarked loftily. Howe nodded in agreement, although he was beginning to think Hilda's care excessive.

Now at last the moment had come. Hilda squinted into the

camera, moved the tripod slightly. She stood to the side, holding the plunger of the shutter-cable. "Ready," she said. "Will you relax, Joseph, please?" Howe realized that he was standing frozen. Hilda stood poised and precise as a setter, one hand holding the little cable, the other extended with curled dainty fingers like a dancer's, as if expressing to her subject the precarious delicacy of the moment. She pressed the plunger and there was the click. At once she stirred to action, got behind the camera, turned a new exposure. "Thank you," she said. "Would you stand under that tree and let me do a character study with light and shade?"

The childish absurdity of the remark restored Howe's ease. He went to the little tree. The pattern the leaves made on his gown was what Hilda was after. He had just taken a satisfactory position when he heard in the unmistakable voice, "Ah, Doctor! Having your picture taken?"

Howe gave up the pose and turned to Blackburn who stood on the walk, his hands behind his back, a little too large for his bachelor's gown. Annoyed that Blackburn should see him posing for a character study in light and shade, Howe said irritably, "Yes, having my picture taken."

Blackburn beamed at Hilda. "And the little photographer," he said. Hilda fixed her eyes on the ground and stood closer to her brilliant and aggressive camera. Blackburn, teetering on his heels, his hands behind his back, wholly prelatical and benignly patient, was not abashed at the silence. At last Howe said, "If you'll excuse us, Mr. Blackburn, we'll go on with the picture."

"Go right ahead, sir. I'm running along." But he only came closer. "Dr. Howe," he said fervently, "I want to tell you how glad I am that I was able to satisfy your standards at last."

Howe was surprised at the hard insulting brightness of his own voice and even Hilda looked up curiously as he said, "Nothing you have ever done has satisfied me and nothing you could ever do would satisfy me, Blackburn."

With a glance at Hilda, Blackburn made a gesture as if to hush Howe—as though all his former bold malice had taken for granted a kind of understanding between himself and his teacher, a secret which must not be betrayed to a third person. "I only meant, sir," he said, "that I was able to pass your course after all."

Howe said, "You didn't pass my course. I passed you out of my course. I passed you without even reading your paper. I wanted to be sure the college would be rid of you. And when all the grades were in and I did read your paper, I saw I was right not to have read it first."

Blackburn presented a stricken face. "It was very bad, sir?"

But Howe had turned away. The paper had been fantastic. The paper had been, if he wished to see it so, mad. It was at this moment that the Dean came up behind Howe and caught his arm. "Hello, Joseph," he said. "We'd better be getting along, it's almost late."

He was not a familiar man, but when he saw Blackburn, who approached to greet him, he took Blackburn's arm, too. "Hello, Theodore," he said. Leaning forward on Howe's arm and on Blackburn's, he said, "Hello, Hilda dear." Hilda replied quietly, "Hello, Uncle George."

Still clinging to their arms, still linking Howe and Blackburn, the Dean said, "Another year gone, Joe, and we've turned out another crop. After you've been here a few years, you'll find it reasonably upsetting—you wonder how there can be so many graduating classes while you stay the same. But of course you don't stay the same." Then he said, "Well," sharply, to dismiss the thought. He pulled Blackburn's arm and swung him around to Howe. "Have you heard about Teddy Blackburn?" he asked. "He has a job already, before graduation, the first man of his class to be placed." Expectant of congratulations, Blackburn beamed at Howe. Howe remained silent.

"Isn't that good?" the Dean said. Still Howe did not answer and the Dean, puzzled and put out, turned to Hilda. "That's a very fine-looking camera, Hilda." She touched it with affectionate pride.

"Instruments of precision," said a voice. "Instruments of precision." Of the three with joined arms, Howe was the nearest to Tertan, whose gaze took in all the scene except the smile and the nod which Howe gave him. The boy leaned on his cane. The broad-brimmed hat, canting jauntily over his eye, confused the image of his face that Howe had established, suppressed the rigid lines of the ascetic and brought out the baroque curves. It made an effect of perverse majesty.

"Instruments of precision," said Tertan for the last time, addressing no one, making a casual comment to the universe. And it occurred to Howe that Tertan might not be referring to Hilda's equipment. The sense of the thrice-woven circle of the boy's loneliness smote him fiercely. Tertan stood in majestic jauntiness, superior to all the scene, but his isolation made Howe ache with a pity of which Tertan was more the cause than the object, so general and indiscriminate was it.

Whether in his sorrow he made some unintended movement toward Tertan which the Dean checked or whether the suddenly tightened grip on his arm was the Dean's own sorrow and fear, he did not know. Tertan watched them in the incurious way people watch a photograph being taken and suddenly the thought that, to the boy, it must seem that the three were posing for a picture together made Howe detach himself almost rudely from the Dean's grasp.

"I promised Hilda another picture," he announced—needlessly, for Tertan was no longer there, he had vanished in the last sudden flux of visitors who, now that the band had struck up, were rushing nervously to find seats.

"You'd better hurry," the Dean said. "I'll go along, it's getting late for me." He departed and Blackburn walked stately by his side.

Howe again took his position under the little tree which cast its shadow over his face and gown. "Just hurry, Hilda, won't you?" he said. Hilda held the cable at arm's length, her other arm crooked and her fingers crisped. She rose on her toes and said "Ready," and pressed the release. "Thank you," she said gravely and began to dismantle her camera as he hurried off to join the procession.